THE COWBOY'S
Mixed-Up Matchmaker

VALERIE COMER

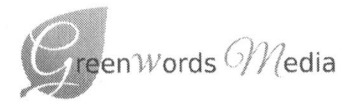

GreenWords Media

Copyright © 2018 Valerie Comer
All rights reserved.
Digital ISBN: 9781988068398
Paperback ISBN: 9781988068404

No part of this publication may be reproduced or transmitted for commercial purposes, except for brief quotations in printed or electronic reviews, without written permission of the author.

This is a work of fiction set in a fictional western Montana. Businesses and locations are used fictitiously. Any resemblance to actual persons, living or dead, is coincidental.

Cover Art © 2018 Lynnette Bonner, www.indiecoverdesign.com.

Cover images purchased from Deposit Photos and Shutterstock

The lyrics to *Be Thou My Vision* are found in the public domain.

The Holy Bible, English Standard Version. ESV® Permanent Text Edition® (2016). Copyright © 2001 by Crossway Bibles, a publishing ministry of Good News Publishers. All rights reserved.

Holy Bible, New International Version®, NIV® Copyright ©1973, 1978, 1984, 2011 by Biblica, Inc.® Used by permission. All rights reserved worldwide.

First edition, GreenWords Media, 2018

Valerie Comer Bibliography

Urban Farm Fresh Romance
0. Promise of Peppermint (ebook only)
1. Secrets of Sunbeams
2. Butterflies on Breezes
3. Memories of Mist
4. Wishes on Wildflowers
5. Flavors of Forever
6. Raindrops on Radishes
7. Dancing at Daybreak

Saddle Springs Romance
1. The Cowboy's Christmas Reunion
2. The Cowboy's Mixed-Up Matchmaker
3. The Cowboy's Romantic Dreamer
4. The Cowboy's Convenient Marriage

Christmas in Montana Romance
1. More Than a Tiara
2. Other Than a Halo
3. Better Than a Crown

Garden Grown Romance
(Arcadia Valley Romance)
1. Sown in Love (ebook only)
2. Sprouts of Love
3. Rooted in Love
4. Harvest of Love

Farm Fresh Romance
1. Raspberries and Vinegar
2. Wild Mint Tea
3. Sweetened with Honey
4. Dandelions for Dinner
5. Plum Upside Down
6. Berry on Top

Riverbend Romance Novellas
1. Secretly Yours
2. Pinky Promise
3. Sweet Serenade
4. Team Bride
5. Merry Kisses

valeriecomer.com/books

Chapter 1

"Did you hear Denae Archibald is coming back to town?"

James Carmichael stifled a groan. Why wouldn't his long-time friend let up trying to find him a date? The closer he got to thirty, the more determined she seemed. On the flip side, the closer he got to thirty, the less interested he was in her games.

"Everything looks good." Lauren Yanovich stripped off her gloves and glanced up at him as she patted Snowball's flank.

"Uh..." Was Lauren talking as a veterinarian about the pregnant horse... or about Denae? It was never safe to assume. James tore his gaze from Lauren and stroked the filly's forelock. "Great. Glad to hear it."

"Denae is a sought-after editor now. Who knew, right? But she was always so good at everything she put her mind to." Lauren lathered up in the stable's deep sink.

"I haven't spent two minutes in the past decade wondering what happened to Denae."

Lauren chuckled but didn't look up. "That's because you haven't seen her lately. She's thin like a model and drop-dead gorgeous. She was even first runner-up at the Miss Snowflake contest over in Helena last Christmas."

"I'm thrilled for her." Hopefully, the bland way he said the words would hush Lauren up.

"You should be. She's going to be renting the other half of my duplex from me starting April first—"

"Ah ha, an April Fool's joke. Nice one, Lauren."

She dried her hands on a scrap of old towel, glancing at James as she shook her head. "You're not getting any younger."

He shrugged. Didn't he know it. Most guys probably dreaded the big three-oh but, for him, it presented an opportunity. A crossroads. His gut roiled at the thought. He should probably purchase shares in an antacid company, with the amount he was going through lately. Or at least buy them by the case. If only he could do something about the situation now, but it was bad timing. It was always a bad time when Lauren focused on matchmaking. He followed her outside, like a pup after a scent.

Lauren rested both arms on the corral rails and took a deep breath as she gazed toward the mountains. "I always love coming out to the Flying Horseshoe. It's so peaceful."

"You say that like Saddle Springs is a big city," he teased. "When we're full-up here in the summer, the ranch's population nearly rivals the town's." She was right, though. His parents' ranch lay tucked in the foothills of western Montana, rolling and picturesque with its small lake. Good thing they'd been able to repurpose the vast acres from working ranch to guest ranch after Dad's accident when James was in college. He'd quit, coming home to pitch in. Never regretted it for a minute. This was his home. His destiny.

"You know what I mean."

He braced beside her, allowing the sleeve of his denim shirt to brush against her navy coveralls. He couldn't feel her arm through all that fabric. Even less when she shifted slightly away.

"I get it." All of it. He stared up to where a few dark clouds shrouded the peaks. Snow again? It was never too late, not in the mountains. They'd even had a dusting in July that one year. Thankfully his best bud's outdoor wedding had gone off without a hitch last weekend.

That only reminded James of Lauren wearing a fitted calf-length turquoise dress, carrying a bouquet of sunny daffodils and white tulips down the grassy aisle. He couldn't remember the last time he'd seen her in a dress. Prom, maybe? At any rate, he hadn't been able to tear his eyes away.

Ask her out already, dude. His friend's voice rang in his memory.

James glanced at Lauren. Her short dark hair curled around her head, a sensible cut for a veterinarian. The coveralls were sensible, too. The jeans and baggy sweatshirts she usually wore probably fit the same label. When had the life of their high school class become *sensible*?

"There's a new waitress at the Branding Iron. Pretty

with long blond hair."

Obviously there was no way Lauren would go out with James. She did everything to get rid of even his friendship. He scowled at her. "Yeah? Why are you telling me this?"

"Because you're—"

"Stop reminding me of my age."

She pulled back at the harshness in his voice. "Sor*ree*. Just trying to help."

"Don't. Just don't."

"I thought you'd probably want to get married and have a batch of little cowpokes running around to keep your nephew company."

"Maybe someday."

She bit her lip. Her pretty, full lip. The one he craved to taste.

"Besides, what about you?" James trod on dangerous ground, now. He didn't actually want to push her away, but her matchmaking needed to stop. Like, yesterday.

"Me?" Lauren tossed her head. "Too busy. With the expansion of the Saddle View subdivision, we've got dozens more horses in the area, many with inexperienced owners. Lots of calls out that way, to say nothing of the usual."

He hated to see her overworked and tired. "Is Doc Torrington putting too much pressure on you? Maybe you guys should hire another vet."

"No, we're good. I've got nothing else to do with my time."

"If you had more time, you could date."

Lauren laughed. "Back around, are we?"

"Well, yeah. As you keep telling me, thirty's coming. As I recall, we share a birthday." Like he'd ever forgotten.

"Maybe we should have a party!" Her hazel eyes sparkled.

"A... what?"

"Surely you've heard of parties. Where a bunch of friends get together and have a good time, often to celebrate a special occasion?"

What he really had in mind was a private dinner for two where he offered his heart in completion of the pledge he'd made on their sixteenth birthday, just after Dillon Scarborough had broken up with her. She'd been crushed.

Good friends don't let friends turn thirty... single.

They'd even high-fived on it.

Even then, he'd adored the ground she walked on. He'd never dreamed that thirteen-and-a-half years later, he might have the chance to redeem his pledge.

She'd probably turn him down. Laugh in his face. She didn't want to marry anyone. She constantly pushed him toward someone else. But, didn't a guy have to try?

Everything on the line.

He'd been working toward the final test of that motto forever.

If he only knew.

Right. Lauren muffled a snort. If he did, he'd laugh his head off, and she couldn't bear that. Nope, her best bet was to carry on as she'd begun, trying to find James's perfect match. When he was safely married off, she could relax — yeah, sure — and focus on her work. She'd even teach his kids in Sunday School, no problem.

Okay, it would be a problem, but she'd do it anyway, because Saddle Springs was home, and she wasn't going anywhere. Neither, apparently, was he. Somebody needed to get married and put her out of her misery. Had to be him.

James's sister came around the corner of the stable, leading a black gelding. "Hey, Lauren."

Whew. Good diversion. "Hiya, Tori. Good-looking boy. He new here?"

Tori nodded. "His name is Coaldust. We just picked him up from a ranch over near Polson."

Lauren took in the gelding's conformation and bright eyes. "How old is he?"

"Five. Saddle broke with an easy gait. I think he'll be a favorite with guests this summer."

Coaldust tossed his head with a little whinny.

Lauren dug in her pocket for the apple chunk left over from Snowball and held it out to Coaldust. He eyed her as though to determine whether she was friend or foe before nipping it off her palm. She rubbed his velvety nose and crooned soft nothings to him as his ears twitched.

As fidgety as James shifting at her side. He was sure

acting odd today... or was he? He'd slid into somewhat moody and unpredictable behavior over the past few months, or maybe even longer. They used to talk for hours, about anything and everything. Well, nearly. A girl needed her secrets. But things had changed, and she couldn't figure out why.

At first, Lauren had thought he'd fallen in love and was thus avoiding her. She'd braced herself for the introduction to his girlfriend and seeing his eyes light up for the other woman, but time went on, and it hadn't happened. It needed to happen, as much as she dreaded it. Once he'd moved on, she could, too. Right?

"...wouldn't that be fun?"

Lauren blinked, refocusing on Tori. "Um, sorry. Wool-gathering. What did you say?"

"Never mind," James said quickly. "Bad idea."

"I think it's a great idea." Tori pouted at her brother and turned back to Lauren. "I was thinking a few of us should get together for a weekend getaway before the summer rush begins. We could ride way back above the Flying Horseshoe and into the National Forest. Camp for a couple of days by the geothermal pool." She elbowed Lauren. "I'll share my tent with you."

James's face shuttered. "There's too much going on."

What on earth was he thinking? Lauren angled a look at him. "It was a ton of fun when we used to do it." So many good memories from before he became owly.

He shrugged.

Men. Lauren turned to Tori. "Let me know what

weekend you're looking at, and I'll see if I can book it off. Who all are you thinking of inviting?"

Tori glanced between them. "Well, us three, of course. We could ask Cheri and Kade. I think Sawyer Delgado is away on the rodeo circuit, but Trevor might be interested."

Trevor would most likely cast a wet blanket on the trip, but that was no more than James was already doing. Who could be counted on for amusement? "Oh, I bet Denae Archibald would love to come. She's moving back April first."

James groaned.

"Nice. And maybe Carmen Haviland?" Tori tapped her jaw. "Possibly Garret Morrison."

"Sounds like a fun group. Are you thinking of including the little ones? Cheri and Kade can probably get his mom to watch their kids, but I'm not sure whether Carmen can get away."

"I can't believe you're talking as though this is a real thing."

Tori jammed her elbow into her brother's side. "Why not? I only got to go along that one time and then you guys quit doing it. Before that, I was just the little tagalong no one wanted."

"We were all kids then."

Lauren chuckled. "I'm pretty sure I'm not too old or out-of-shape to sit in the saddle for a few hours on a mountain trail. If *you* are..."

He scowled at her. "You don't know what you're talking about, woman."

"Well, either you can handle trail riding, or you can't."

"It's not about being horseback."

She raised her eyebrows, not daring to read anything into his piercing glare. "Then what? I happen to know you can cook."

"I have to say he's out of practice." Tori giggled.

He whooshed out a long breath and looked between them. "I just want to go on record as saying it's a bad idea. Okay?" Then he strode away.

She dared watch his fine form until he disappeared into the end guest cabin he'd claimed for his own a couple of years ago, the scuffed boots, snug jeans, denim shirt stretched over broad shoulders, and his dark cowboy hat etched in her memory along with all the other sightings.

"Man, he's like a bear stumbling out of a leaky cave in the middle of winter," Tori observed. "He's been such a grouch for the past few months. Even worse since Kade and Cheri's wedding. Wasn't that dreamy?" She sighed. "Talk about a happy ending."

"James is probably pining for a good love story of his own," Lauren said lightly. "I was thinking he and Denae might hit it off, so your idea of a camping trip is great timing."

Tori tilted her head and regarded Lauren. "Interesting thought. I've sometimes wondered why he hasn't latched onto a gorgeous woman of his own. I mean, the grumpiness is off-putting, I'm sure, but he's decently good-looking. If a kid sister is allowed to say so."

"I've seen uglier. At least he doesn't have a wart on his

nose." Lauren forced out a chuckle. "He probably just hasn't met the right girl yet. When he does, he'll move so quickly your head will spin."

Tori giggled. "You're probably right. So, what's your work schedule like? How many weekends do you get off? Then I'll start calling around to see who's in, and we'll go from there."

Lauren pulled out her phone and opened the calendar app, sharing the info with Tori.

"Great. I'll be in touch." Tori thumbed over her shoulder toward James's cabin. "And if Mr. Grumpy doesn't want to come along, we can have a great time without him."

"Yeah! We sure can." Lauren slapped Tori's raised palm. "I'd better get back to the clinic and see what other calls we've got. Keep me in the loop."

"Will do."

Lauren climbed into her Jeep Wrangler and shot one more glance at James's cabin. A good time camping without him? Definitely not. There'd be a huge gap if he didn't come. It wasn't just his voice lifted around the campfire during the sing-along she'd miss. She'd miss his easy way in the forest, building a fire, helping everyone out with all the little things in camp, making everything run smoothly. She'd miss filling her eyes and mind with his handsome — if somewhat moody — face.

No. What she'd really miss was the chance to hook him up with Denae.

Chapter 2

"So, Mom. A bunch of us are thinking of taking a backcountry trip the weekend before Memorial Day. Would you guys manage okay if both James and I were gone for three or four days?"

James lowered his fork and stared at the beef stew in front of him. One night he could almost fathom. Three or four, with Lauren nearby trying to foist him off on some other woman? No way.

"That sounds fun. You make me wish I were young again."

Not that Mom would ever go without Dad, and his legs were too gimped from the accident to ride. A rancher who couldn't ride. What could be a worse fate?

"I'm not sure I can take that long, actually." James glowered at his kid sister. "There's a lot to do before it gets crazy in late May." Cozy family dinners would be at an end when the summer staff arrived. The seasonal restaurant would be open, and he wouldn't have to put up with Tori so much. Sure, she'd grown up to be a big help around the Flying Horseshoe Guest Ranch, but that didn't keep her from being far too nosy for her own good.

She waved her hand. "You've got nearly two months to get everything prepared, and I bet Meg and Eli can fill in some that weekend. Lauren says she can take the Thursday through Sunday off." Tori slathered butter on homemade sourdough bread.

"Lauren's going?" Dad asked, voice casual.

James felt his dad's sidelong glance. No point meeting it.

"Yep." Tori took a big bite before continuing. "She's inviting Denae Archibald, and some others are considering it. I made a few phone calls this afternoon. I think there'll be six or eight of us."

Not big enough numbers for safety. The closer the big three-oh loomed, the more nervous James got. He'd find out how out-of-control his dreams had grown when he dropped to one knee and asked Lauren to marry him. She'd laugh. He knew she would, but he'd meant what he'd said the night of their sixteenth. He'd never forgotten, even if all evidence pointed to the fact that she'd never taken it seriously. He was a man who kept his word, but this one wouldn't be a hardship.

James shoveled a forkful of stew in his mouth. A moment before, the aroma had been mouth-watering, the flavors delectable. Now it was no better than a lump of dog food. The black Lab sprawled over by the door didn't know how close he was to a plateful of people food, but Brody wouldn't need more than one invitation.

"I ran into Gloria in town this morning." Mom took a sip of iced tea. "They excavated the foundation of Kade and Cheri's house yesterday."

"Are they back from their honeymoon?" Tori sighed. "That was the most romantic wedding ever."

"The kids are flying in tomorrow, she said."

Things would never be the same with his best friend remarried. James was happy for Kade. He was. Really. It just made him feel more like a loser himself. What guy staring down the barrel at thirty had only dated a handful of times? One with a plan, he reminded himself. A plan with as many holes in it as the targets he and Kade had practiced shooting their .22s at as kids.

"I've been thinking, son."

James pulled his attention over to his dad. "Yes, sir?" Probably some new idea for the guest ranch. They needed constant innovation to keep their edge as a prime tourist destination.

"Have you thought of building your own place? That little meadow near Meg and Eli's on the other side of the lake would be a great building site. Not too far from utility hookups."

James stared at Dad and snapped his gaping mouth shut. "Uh, no. I hadn't given it any thought." Why now? "Are we turning away too many guests because I have one of the guest cabins? Maybe we should invest in several more of those rather than an actual house." A house for one guy.

Dad waved a hand. "No, no. I mean, that's not a bad

idea, but it isn't the reason." He glanced at Mom, who smiled at James.

Great. This wasn't some off-hand suggestion.

"Your mother reminded me that you're soon to be thirty. I'd somehow thought you might bring home a great girl sometime and we'd hear wedding bells. The guest cabin was supposed to be a stop-gap measure for a young man who didn't need parental supervision, not something long-term."

"Ooh! If Jamie builds a house, can I have his cabin?"

Trust Tori to seek an advantage. But then, what twenty-five-year-old wanted to live with her parents? He couldn't blame her. Still, the cabin was a great size for a single guy who rarely cooked. He often ate with his folks or, during the busy season, in the ranch dining room.

"Gloria was saying they'd hired Timber Framing Plus out of Coeur d'Alene," Mom went on. "They have a great reputation in the Inland Northwest for custom homes with quality work."

"Yes, Kade showed me their website, and I went with him to see a couple of their houses up near Libby one day." That wasn't the shock. The surprise was his parents' thoughts that he should do the same... but without a wife. Kade had lived in the apartment above his parents' garage until his marriage to Cheri. James had figured he'd do the same. Keep doing what he was doing until something changed. At least he wasn't saddled with a baby like Kade had been.

Did he actually have the nerve to follow through? He'd spent over a decade being one of Lauren's best friends while hiding his feelings for her since she didn't seem to reciprocate. How many evenings had they leaned against the corral rails talking into the wee hours? Sat on bales in the stable, sharing their thoughts? Or out by a bonfire?

It was comfortable. At least, when he was able to ignore the deep longing for more. She wasn't ready. He knew that. But would she ever be?

Or was it him just being chicken?

"You work too hard."

Nothing like coming home after a long day to discover her mother in her kitchen with a bag of takeout. The chicken at least was welcome. Even Felix-the-cat sat at attention, drooling.

Lauren pushed out a tired smile. "Just doing my job. I knew being a veterinarian wouldn't be like a nine-to-five office job. I saw Dad's crazy hours when I was growing up."

Mom's lips pursed. "At least there is no such thing as an emergency haircut."

And here they were again. Yeah, her mom made a decent living as owner of Shear Inspirations in downtown Saddle Springs, but the thought of becoming a hair stylist working for her mother had fled screaming out of Lauren's head almost before it had entered. She'd been a daddy's girl, hanging around the vet clinic and going out on calls with him as often as he'd let her... much to her mother's dismay. If only Dad hadn't died before Lauren could take her place beside him in the practice he and his best friend, Wyatt Torrington, had built from the ground up.

"I love my job, Mom. Let me grab a quick shower and be right with you. Thanks for bringing dinner."

Mom glared at the clock on the back of the stove. "It will be cold by then."

It was probably cold already, if Mom had been here since five o'clock. Lena Yang had brought her kids' puppy in at quarter to after a tangle with barbed wire. "I won't be long. Besides, that's why God invented microwaves."

"Don't be heretical."

Lauren grinned and fluttered her fingers as she left the tiny kitchen.

Behind her, Mom muttered something about being a better example to the children she taught in Sunday school.

No going back to argue the point. Also, no hoping Mom would have gone home by the time Lauren had sluiced the day's grime off her body, no matter how long Lauren stayed under the scalding spray.

A few minutes later she wandered back into the kitchen in gray sweats.

Mom narrowed her gaze as she examined her daughter. "If that's your idea of evening attire, no wonder you can't catch a man."

"Evening attire? Let's call it comfy casual. I'm not looking for a man." Lauren opened the bag of takeout, taking a deep whiff of fried chicken as she plated it.

"Being alone all your life isn't any way to live."

She popped the plate into the microwave and dished out the coleslaw. "Don't bother, Mom."

Her mother huffed. "Don't bother what? Caring about my only child? The only person I have left on the planet?"

"I'm sorry I don't meet your expectations, but I'm honestly happy the way I am. I love my work, and I have lots of friends." The microwave beeped. Lauren lifted out the plate and carried it to the table, nearly tripping over Felix, then dipped her head and said grace aloud while there was still a lull.

Hmm. How to divert attention from herself? "Did I tell you Denae Archibald is going to be renting the other half of the duplex from me?"

"You told me." Mom pursed her lips. "That family has too much money."

Ahh. Mom took the bait. Perfect. "Her dad's a lawyer and her stepmom's a high-profile IT consultant. They earned their wealth the old-fashioned way."

"Denae's spoiled."

Lauren dug into her chicken. Despite the unwelcome sight of her mom, not having to think about dinner was a pleasant relief.

Mom picked the skin off a piece of poultry and set it aside. "She's too skinny. Do you think she's anorexic?"

"No, I doubt it. She simply has a very revved metabolism." Lauren reached for a second piece of chicken but hesitated. Did she eat too much? Was that why her clothes fit more snugly than they had last year?

Not that the coleslaw was likely a better option, doused with enough dressing to drown a cat. *Sorry, Felix. You can have the skin off Mom's drum.* She pushed her plate away.

Mom frowned. "You need to keep up your energy. Eat."

Maybe a second piece would at least keep the tummy rumbles at bay. She really needed to get better at planning ahead with healthy options. Not that the internet — or her friends — agreed what those were. Low fat? Low carb? Weight Watchers? Whole30? Trim Healthy Mama? At least the days of the cabbage cleanse were over.

That meant the coleslaw was definitely out.

"So, did you have any calls out today?"

"A couple," mumbled Lauren around the meat.

"Tell me."

Her mom had been practiced at conversation with a veterinarian. "A calf with an abscessed leg up at Eaglecrest, but she'll be okay." She should give Russ Delgado a call and make sure. "And then I checked in at the Flying Horseshoe. They have a mare about to foal for the first time, so I've been keeping an eye on her."

Mom narrowed her gaze at Lauren.

Great. Here came the other barrel.

"I wonder why James has never married. Or even Victoria, though she's much younger than her brother."

"Guess neither of them has met the right person yet." Lauren gathered the dishes from the table, rinsed them, and slotted them in the dishwasher. By Friday it might be worth running the load.

"Kids these days, living at home until they're thirty. Does no one want to grow up?"

Lauren forced a chuckle. "Maybe being an adult is overrated." Not that James wasn't a mature, grown man. The way he filled out his denim shirt, the short, trimmed beard... everything about him screamed testosterone. "Besides, he doesn't exactly live at home. He has his own cabin. It's just that he works for his parents. Why should he commute from town every day?"

Mom harrumphed.

How much longer would she stay? These random drop-ins had become more frequent. More stressful. Lauren could use a bit of time to decompress before bed. She had a romance novel with her name on it. Sadly, it didn't have her name *in* it.

"I thought maybe the two of you would fall in love one day."

So had Lauren. They'd both been wrong. "Nope. Sorry to disappoint you." And even more sorry to disappoint herself, but what could she do about it? She'd tried to drop a hint or two a few years ago, but he either hadn't caught it, or ignoring it was his preferred option. Above all, she didn't want to lose his friendship, the easy camaraderie they shared.

So, her best bet was to get him married off. Then she could relax and see what came next for her. Until James Carmichael was tied up in matrimonial knots, her desperate heart could keep pining. James needed to fall in love. That was all there was to it.

She scooped up Felix and turned back to her mother. "Have you been down to the Branding Iron lately?"

Mom frowned. "I have not, and you shouldn't, either. It's a pub."

"Bar and grill," corrected Lauren. "It's not the only restaurant in town that serves liquor along with food. Really good food, I might add."

Silence.

Alrighty then. "I only wondered if you knew who the new waitress is. She's very pretty and seems friendly."

"Working at a place like that, you have to know what *friendly* means."

"Oh, good grief, Mom. Don't even start. I meant friendly in the normal way. Someone with a happy smile and a cheery voice. It was busy the night I was in there, so I didn't get a chance to find out more about her."

"Why do you care?"

"Why not? I know everyone in Saddle Springs. I don't know her. So, if she's new, she probably doesn't have many friends here. No one should be alone unless they want to be."

Mom shook her head. "If you spent half as much time considering your own future as you do everyone else's..."

Enough. "It's only seven thirty. I might pop by there for a little while and see if she's working." Her book and bed could wait.

"Well, I know when I'm not wanted." Mom pulled to her feet. "Mark my words, you need to think a little about life balance. Thirty is just around the corner."

Lauren managed a smile. "I know. It's kind of an exciting prospect. Don't you think?"

Yep, that was enough to get her mother pointed at the door. "Get out of your pajamas before you go in public."

Pajamas? Lauren looked down. She was wearing sweats, not pjs. She was fine.

Chapter 3

A flicker of unease poked at James in the wee hours a few nights later. Hadn't he checked Snowball not two hours earlier to find her resting comfortably? But he couldn't get the approaching birth out of his mind. Best thing to do was yank on some clothes and check her again. And again, if need be. It wouldn't be the first time he'd lost sleep over a horse, and it wouldn't be the last.

He stifled a yawn as he jammed his feet into boots and plopped his hat on his head. Brody perked up in the corner and followed him outside, game for an excursion at any time of day or night, no matter how cold. Stars glittered in the night sky, but the moon wasn't visible.

James tugged open the stable door to the familiar aroma of horses and hay, and soft sounds as several of the animals moved around their roomy stalls. He turned on low-level lights. Swishing his tail, Brody led the way to Snowball's stall.

The horse faced the gate but ignored his arrival. She panted slightly then strained.

The vestiges of sleep fled. James opened the gate and slipped inside the stall, circling to the filly's other end. With that amount of pushing, a hoof or two should be visible, but no.

Not good. Sure, Snowball could be in the earliest stage of labor, but then she shouldn't sound so tired. James fumbled in his pocket, yanked out his phone, and tapped Lauren's number. He hated to wake her, but morning could be too late.

"Hello?"

"Hey. Snowball's in labor and not progressing."

Lauren's voice snapped awake. "Be there in ten."

"Thanks." Should he wake his father? Before the accident, he would have. Now Dad was a well of information, but little physical help. No. Lauren had way more training and would be here in no time. No need to interrupt anyone else's sleep. He shoved the phone back in his pocket.

This time when Snowball strained, the tip of one hoof peeked out for a few seconds.

Maybe he'd called prematurely. Maybe Lauren would come in just in time to greet the foal. At least she wouldn't be angry at the wasted call. She'd bill him — as she should — but she wouldn't be mad.

The hoof retreated.

Good thing Lauren was coming, but he should prepare for the worst. He left the stall and stripped off his shirt. The chill would soon be forgotten… he hoped. Meanwhile, he scrubbed his upper body, arms, and hands with disinfectant. If Lauren needed an assistant, he'd be ready.

Donny Jones knew better than to stop a speeding veterinarian at two in the morning. The state patroller waved as Lauren zipped past. She roared the Wrangler up beside the Flying Horseshoe's stable and cut the engine.

Eight minutes.

Some kind of record, even for her. She grabbed her coveralls and medical bag out of the back and jogged for the stable.

The door swung open, revealing James's silhouette against the low light inside. He'd be a good person to have on her side if things went south in the next little while. Steady. Patient. Intuitive. She wouldn't need the other veterinarian in her practice.

Hopefully.

Oh, man. The guy wasn't wearing a shirt. No matter how much she wanted to stare at the rippling muscles in his torso and arms, she couldn't. "How is she?" She brushed past. At least he smelled more of disinfectant than of his usual manly scent.

"One hoof protruding. I'm guessing the other leg is folded back, but I haven't dug in to look." He followed her down the passageway as he spoke. "I was about to do that."

"I've got it." Lauren stepped into her coveralls then rolled a long disposable glove-and-sleeve combo up her arm. "Disinfectant?"

He dribbled the liquid down her right arm, swabbing the entire area.

She closed her eyes and held still, trying not to react to his proximity. Nearly impossible. Then she turned to the wide-eyed horse. "Hey, Snowball. You're not even going to notice this…"

James let out a short chuckle as he rubbed his hands over the horse's head. So much for the disinfectant, but the touch seemed to comfort Snowball. It ought to. It would certainly have that effect on every other red-blooded female on the planet, Lauren included.

No time for that, though. She reached past the hoof in the birth canal, searching for the other one. Instead, her fingers met the foal's nose. A little more groping, and she found the bent knee.

"You're right. Incomplete elbow extension. I need to repel the fetal trunk to give room for repositioning."

"What do you need me to do?"

"Keep her calm. And pray."

"You've got it."

His soft prayers over Snowball soothed Lauren, too. She hadn't done this maneuver without Wyatt watching over her before. The other vet had been her dad's partner and had nearly forty years' experience. Maybe she should have called him as she jumped in the Jeep. But, no, she had the training. She knew what to do, and her hands were smaller than Wyatt's. She could do this, but if there was any client she didn't want to let down, it was James.

Lord, help me.

She waited until the contraction eased before reaching in once again and applying persistent pressure to the shoulder. Push, push. She wouldn't have long before nature worked against her. She held steady, gritting her teeth, through the next contraction, then pushed further down the birth canal until the foal lay back in the uterus.

Time stood still. Snowball whimpered. James sang *Rock of Ages* in a low, steady voice. Lauren groped for the other hoof, found it, and drew it forward. Double checked the foal's nose was in place. Withdrew her arm.

And waited, holding her breath, for the next contraction.

A hoof protruded, then the second one, then the nose.

Lauren sagged against the board-and-batten wall of the stall, gaze pinned to the action.

"All is well?" James leaned beside her, arms crossed over his chest.

"The next few minutes will tell." The guy must be freezing. She certainly wasn't, but she'd been working hard and pumping serious adrenaline.

"You did good."

"You don't know that yet."

He nudged her shoulder, and she closed her eyes, drinking in the contact, trying not to remember his bare skin. At least *she* was wearing several layers.

"There it comes."

Lauren blinked and refocused just as the foal whooshed from the birth canal and slithered to the hay. Snowball turned and nuzzled her baby. James dropped to his knees beside it, grabbed a handful of straw, and wiped the mucus from the newborn's nose. The little one shook its head as though to get away from the scratchy substance.

James sat back on his heels and watched as the foal struggled to its feet.

Lauren leaned on the wall and watched James. It wasn't like she'd never seen him shirtless before. The gang had often swum in the little lake on the Flying Horseshoe and floated down the river in inner tubes, but this was the first time the sight affected her this way. Made her want to slide her fingertips over his shoulders, play with the hair at the nape of his neck, touch the curls feathering his chest.

She needed to focus on something else. Anything else. She couldn't.

He glanced up and caught her staring, and something darkened in his eyes before he looked away. Probably saw the truth in her eyes and was repulsed by it.

Lauren knelt in the straw on the other side of the foal. "Colt or filly?"

"Filly," he answered.

But of course, she had to check for herself. Check all the vitals. The little gal seemed well for all the trauma surrounding her birth.

Lauren stripped the disposable sleeve down her arm, rolled it up, and tucked it into a trash bag. She should head home now. James was well able to monitor the newborn while waiting for Snowball to pass her placenta. The situation didn't call for two anymore.

She didn't want to leave. This was, by far, the most intimate half hour she'd ever spent with James, unless she counted the pledge of the sixteen-year-old who vowed not to let her be thirty and single.

Yeah, well, if he'd actually meant that, things would have turned out much differently, wouldn't they? Yes. Yes, they would. He'd have wooed her like Kade had wooed Cheri back when they were all young adults, pledging undying love rather than a teenage solidarity. Unlike Cheri, Lauren would never have jilted James a week before the wedding.

Not a chance.

Against her wishes, her gaze followed him as he shrugged into his shirt, but she managed to look away as he turned back toward her.

"I wasn't sure if I'd need to get in there myself," he said by way of explanation as he snapped up the front.

It was okay to look at him when he was talking, right? Especially now that he was fully clothed again. "Good thinking. It's best to be prepared."

"I can't thank you enough for coming out here in the middle of the night. In theory, I know what to do, but I've never seen it done before. It was comforting knowing you had the training and experience to back you up."

Was this where she should explain it was her first time solo? Nah. "You can thank me by paying the invoice."

"The minute I get it." He held her gaze.

"That's all I need." Liar. She needed a whole lot more. She needed this man with a near primal urge. A braver Lauren would reach for him, but the veterinarian standing in the stable knew better. Knew it was just the magic of the moment, the teamwork, the low lighting, the gentle swishes of horses' tails, the aroma of the stable, and the late-night hour. All those things together at once.

That's all it was.

Lauren turned away, immediately feeling the loss of contact. She folded the trays of her veterinary case in and snapped it shut.

"Do you want to name her?" James's quiet voice was nearer than she'd expected, and she jumped a little.

"Me?" Lauren looked up at him. So near. So tantalizingly near.

"Sure, why not? She's not purebred or anything like that, so there isn't a standard format. Plus, she might not be here if it weren't for you."

She wanted to demur, but the professional in her wouldn't let her. He'd absolutely done the right thing by calling in a veterinarian. "I-I don't know. I'll have to think about it."

He nodded, his gaze never breaking from hers. "Let me know in the next day or two what you come up with. I imagine you'll swing past again to make sure all is well?"

"Of course." James didn't need to know that was standard practice only for the Flying Horseshoe. She and Wyatt didn't have time to check back on every single call-out. "And do feel free to call if you have any concerns."

A grin crinkled his cheeks and feathered laugh lines from his eyes. "You know I will."

Lauren nodded crisply and looked away. She had to focus elsewhere — like on the fact that dawn was still a couple of hours away — and get off the ranch before she did something really stupid like give James a hug.

She waved once more, stowed her gear, and turned the key in the ignition.

He stood watching her, bathed in the glow of the stable lights, until she rounded a curve and couldn't see him in her mirror anymore.

Then she took a long, shuddering breath. *Get a grip, girl.*

What would happen if she casually said something like, "hey, remember our sixteenth when you promised not to let me turn thirty, still single? Look at us. Here we are..."

That would go over well. His brow would furrow as he stared at her in confusion. Then he'd laugh, dig his elbow into her ribs, and tell her that was a good one. Or else there'd be a flicker of disappointment and pity before he told her he'd honor that pact because of their friendship.

Lauren didn't want a pity proposal. She wanted James on a charger, ready to do battle for the woman he loved passionately. Which was totally a daydream because, if he did love her, he wouldn't be waiting for anything. He'd let her know.

So, he didn't love her. And she needed to get over him.

The thought of trying to figure out how to do that kept her staring at the ceiling until her alarm went off a couple of hours later.

CHAPTER 4

"You should have called me." Dad's eyes clouded with disappointment as he surveyed James across the breakfast table.

Was this where James told his father he was too gimped to help? That didn't seem polite. "I told you, I called Lauren."

"I've turned many a calf and foal in my day."

"Now, Bill, you know you can't do everything you used to." Mom's hand rested on Dad's forearm. "James made the best call he could at two o'clock."

Dad glowered at her, but she didn't pull back. "When I was growing up, we didn't phone the vet for every little thing."

James picked at his omelet. "It wasn't a little thing. The foal's hoof was back. Snowball could have pushed all night and not given birth. They could both have died. I don't think bringing in a veterinarian was a bad choice."

Yeah, he'd totally enjoyed watching Lauren at work.

Sharing the entire experience with her was something he'd willingly pay triple for. The quiet ambience of a stable at night, watching the miracle of birth beside the woman he loved... this night would be entrenched in his memory forever.

But that didn't mitigate the facts. Snowball had been in trouble. Lauren was a vet who could, and did, fix it. They now had a healthy mare and foal. Where was his dad's problem with that? If the guest ranch were in financial trouble, his parents would never have suggested James build a house. If it wasn't that, it was just his dad's ego.

And a man's ego was a fragile thing not to be tampered with. James tried to put himself in his father's well-worn cowboy boots for a moment. His dad had ridden every day, yet those boots had not slid into stirrups in seven years. Everything Bill Carmichael had known had been ripped from him in one death-defying moment. Well, not everything. He'd retained his life, his family, and his ranch, but his day-to-day life had one-eightied in every possible way.

"I'm sorry, Dad. You're right. I should have touched base with you."

Dad settled back into his chair, a slight smile of satisfaction lurking.

Mom gave James a sharp look.

James shrugged and finished his omelet. He could have texted Dad after he'd called Lauren, more as an FYI than anything else. Odds were Dad wouldn't even have heard the subtle chime of an incoming text above his own snoring. Honestly, though? Dad's presence in the stall would have broken the magic. Not that the magic was leading anywhere. The glitter he'd imagined in the air had likely been dust motes.

"What's on the agenda today?" Tori asked.

"Your father is doing call-backs to confirm the summer staff this afternoon." Mom cleared dishes off the table. "I could use a hand with cleaning the staff quarters."

"Someone needs to ride the trails and clear any deadfall. With so many big storms last winter, there's sure to be lot of trees down." Dad eyed James. "Take your chainsaw."

He'd rather stick around HQ today and keep an eye on the foal. He could even handle scrubbing with his mom, but Tori couldn't manage the heavy chainsaw.

"I'll pop in on Snowball often." Tori swatted James's arm. "Have you named the foal yet?"

Generally, whoever was present at a birth got the honors, so it was a reasonable question. "Lauren's thinking about a name."

Tori's eyebrows rose.

James's chair scraped the floor as he stood. "I'll get my things together and grab a mobile phone from the office. Buzz me if there's anything I need to know."

He rummaged in the fridge for leftover roast beef then wedged chunks of it between thick slices of his mom's homemade sourdough bread. Tori had baked oatmeal date cookies yesterday. A handful of those joined the sandwiches in his pack. A thermos of hot coffee and another of cold water went into the pack's side pockets.

Though the day was clear and reasonably pleasant for late March, he stuffed a windbreaker inside, as well.

Outside, he topped off the ATV's tank then strapped an extra jerry can of fuel to the rack beside the chainsaw before running through his mental checklist.

"Which trail are you taking?" Tori stood beside him, arms crossed over her chest, shivering in her light T-shirt and jeans.

"Hooded Mountain. Then I'll circle past the lake and come back down Shedly Creek."

She nodded. "Unless there are more trees down than usual, you should be back before dark."

"Yep. If not, send the posse after me." He straddled the quad and reached for the key.

"Want me to let you know if Lauren comes by?" A singsong quality lit Tori's voice.

What did his sister think she knew? James's hand dropped away from the ignition. "Why would you?"

"She might come to see if you liked her choice of names for the filly."

He shrugged. "She can text me. I'll see it when I'm home."

"Or she might come just to stare dreamily at you."

"As if." He barked a short laugh. "We're just friends. She doesn't see me like that."

Tori sidled closer. "You think?"

"What's with the twenty questions? I've known Lauren since we were in diapers. Pretty sure I'd know if she had a romantic thought in her head."

"You know what I think?"

"No, but I'm sure I'm about to find out."

She grinned and waggled her eyebrows. "I think you two are in love, but no one is willing to make the first move. I also think that's crazy."

"It's *you* who's crazy." James managed a grin he hoped looked amused and carefree. "Turn your imagination to good, not evil." He turned the key, and the quad roared to life. A twist of the throttle, and he rode out of the ranch yard without a second glance back at his sister.

Tori would be the last person he'd confide in. Life hadn't walloped all the romantic notions out of her head yet.

Maybe she'd be one of the lucky ones who wouldn't experience the pain of unrequited love. He wouldn't wish it on anyone.

Lauren turned onto her street at the end of a busy but blessedly uneventful day only to discover Denae's car at the curb. At least she wouldn't spend her evening wondering if that look in James's eyes meant anything. Of course, it didn't. She knew that, so there was no point in contemplating.

Denae erupted off the wicker chair on Lauren's front porch. "Hey! I'm sorry I didn't let you know I was coming today. To make up for it, I want to take you for dinner. Where's good? The Munching Moose?"

"Hey, yourself." Lauren hugged her friend. "The Moose is only open for lunch except in summer. How about The Branding Iron?" That sounded really good, actually. Their ribs were divine. She could taste them already.

"Yeah! Let's do it. Although, girlfriend, you look bagged."

"I was up in the middle of the night to help with a difficult foaling, but I'm good. Not the first time, and it definitely won't be the last in my line of work."

"I couldn't do it." Denae tossed her long black hair over her shoulder. "I need my beauty sleep, or I can't function."

The words *beauty sleep* weren't even in Lauren's vocabulary. She looked down at her scrubs. "Give me a minute to change, and I'll be right with you. Come on in." Maybe the nondescript sweats she usually kicked into after work were not the best choice when going out with Denae, whose slender figure showed off well in skinny yoga pants and a flowy top with angled ruffles.

While Denae waited, Lauren changed into jeans and a blue MSU Bobcats T-shirt, ran a pick through her curls, and gave herself a critical once-over in the mirror. She was lucky Denae deigned to be seen with her. One of these days she really needed to get some new outfits, something more flattering. The thought of a shopping day was as welcome as having a tooth pulled with no anesthetic.

She breezed into the kitchen, freshened Felix's water dish, and grabbed her shoulder bag. "Let's go. I'm starving."

Denae chuckled and led the way out to her RAV4. "Hop in, girlfriend, and let's go find food."

A few minutes later they were seated in a booth in the rustic restaurant where Kenny Chesney belted out his most recent country song. Wait staff in cowboy hats surged from table to table, wearing plaid snap-front shirts tucked into belted jeans.

The new girl stopped at the end of their booth. "Howdy, I'm Anna, and I'm your waitress tonight." She rattled off the evening's special.

Lauren grinned at her. "Good to meet you. I'm Lauren, one of the veterinarians here in Saddle Springs, and this is my friend Denae Archibald, who's moving back to town after a few years away."

"Great." Anna shot a big smile from one to the other. "What can I get you to drink?"

"A diet cola for me, please." Lauren motioned at Denae.

"Ice water. Hold the lemon."

"You've got it." Anna breezed away.

Plain ice water. Lauren should try that sometime. Probably all those soft drinks — diet or otherwise — weren't helping her figure any. Cutting back to water sounded more doable than jogging five miles every day.

Anna returned with their drinks, expectantly holding a pen and pad.

"New in town?" Lauren asked.

"A couple of months. Came over from Bozeman."

"Oh, I went to college there. Do you ride?"

Anna blinked. "As in, horses?"

Denae chuckled. "Welcome to the wild west town of Saddle Springs, where riding means nothing else."

"Um, no. Sorry. Horses are stinky and really, really tall." The waitress made a face. "Are you going to run me out of town now?"

"Not yet." Lauren grinned. "If you're looking for riding lessons, you should check out the Flying Horseshoe Ranch. They've got good mounts for beginners, and James Carmichael is a very patient teacher."

Anna's eyes glazed over and she tapped her pen slightly on the end of the plank table.

"He's also single and cute."

"Did I mention we have ribs on special tonight?"

Okay, so Anna wasn't looking to be set up. "Yes. Sounds good to me. I'll go with honey garlic. They come with French fries and coleslaw, right?"

"Yep. And sticky toffee pudding for dessert."

"Yum." Lauren closed her menu and slid it to the end.

"I'll take the chicken taco salad, and hold the chips, please. Can you serve that with low-fat ranch dressing?"

Oh, man. She should have let Denae order first. Then she wouldn't look like such a glutton in front of her friend.

"Can do." Anna grinned, gathered the menus, and sashayed away to the beat of Vince Gill.

"I wonder what brings a non-rider to Saddle Springs," mused Denae.

"Who knows? Listen, a few of us are planning a trail ride camping trip in mid-May for a few days. Interested in joining us?"

Denae angled her head. "Sounds fun. I haven't done much riding in Missoula, though. I'm sure my rear will be mighty sore."

She certainly had no padding on it. "You've got a few weeks to get in shape for it, if you want to."

"Where at? You mentioned Carmichaels' ranch..."

"Yes, they have a guest ranch now, since Bill's accident. You might have heard about that?"

"My dad told me."

Probably Denae's lawyer dad had sued the pants off the farmer who should have known better than to start an auger when someone was working in the equipment bed. Bill's legs had been caught and mangled before the other guy realized what he'd done and hit the off switch.

"So, the Flying Horseshoe is a great option for riding lessons, at least before summer hits and they're booked up with tourists. Canyon Crossing Stables is another place with rentals. The Morrisons bought that business since you lived here." Should she talk up Garret Morrison? No, she needed to get James Carmichael married off before she got diverted helping anyone else.

"Sounds good. I spend way too much time sitting around on my computer editing manuscripts. The great outdoors is one of the reasons I wanted to move back here from Missoula. I have such good memories of all my visits to Dad's when I was growing up, and I guess I want to recapture some of that."

A shadow fell over the end of the table as a large Stetson blocked the light from the wagon-wheel chandelier. "Hey, Lauren. Thanks for lancing that calf's abscess. I thought you'd like to know his leg is healing up well."

"That's great, Trevor!" Lauren beamed at the oldest Delgado brother. "I was hoping to make it up to Eaglecrest today, but we had a super full day at the clinic."

He nodded. "If you get a chance to check on him, I'd appreciate it. Just to be on the safe side."

Lauren mentally scanned the next day's agenda. "Probably in the afternoon."

"Good." He glanced over at Denae.

"Trevor, you remember Denae Archibald, don't you? Stewy's daughter. She used to spend summers with her dad way back when."

He tipped his hat. "I'd never have recognized you from the scrawny little kid you once were."

Lauren winced at the way he mentioned his memory, but Denae laughed. "Trevor Delgado, right? Your dad bought out my dad's ranch when he and Michelle moved back to Missoula."

"That's right."

"It's even funnier than that," interjected Lauren. "Trevor's actually living in the Standing Rock ranch house."

"It's a lovely family home." Denae gave a wistful sigh.

"Trevor's single."

The cowboy shot her an indecipherable look. Well, it was true, wasn't it? He turned back to Denae. "You want to come up and have a look around sometime for old time's sake, give me a call. It's a real nice place."

"Thanks. I might do that."

Trevor tipped his hat again and stepped back from the table right into Anna's path, sending their drinks sloshing on her tray. "Excuse me, miss."

"It's fine." She smiled up at him. "No harm done." She wiped the glasses with a napkin as she set each on the table. "Your dinner will be right out."

When Lauren looked up, Trevor had disappeared, but Denae stared off into space with a little smile. "Whatcha thinking?"

"Oh, nothing." Denae swirled her glass, clinking the ice. "I can't wait to get moved into the duplex. Dad's driving up the U-Haul Sunday after church. Think we can round up any help to get it offloaded? Like maybe Trevor?" Denae giggled. "I shouldn't even ask. Wow, he's filled out fine since he was a teen."

Lauren needed to get her friend on the same page as her. "I'm sure James will be available. Maybe others." At Denae's raised eyebrows, she stifled a sigh. "I can check with Trevor."

Chapter 5

Remind him again why he couldn't ever turn Lauren down? Here he was, eyes wide open, walking directly into her not-so-invisible trap to set him up with her renter, all because it meant being near her for a few hours... which was all he could handle.

She'd managed to round up most of the gang, though Kade and Cheri had sent their apologies. No surprise. Not only were they just back from their honeymoon, they had two little kids who'd missed their parents and would only be underfoot.

James grunted under the weight of a walnut desk as he and Trevor navigated the narrow staircase's tight turn.

"It's no easier at this end." Trevor glared at him from above, bent over and hands gripping the narrow lip around the polished top.

"I know," growled James. "There isn't any pizza worth this stupid desk."

Humor flickered in the other guy's eyes. "If we leave

it right here, I'll have to jump out an upstairs window, and no one can ever use these stairs again. Might be worth it."

James turned the desk with an eighth of an inch to spare before leaving a scratch on the wall paint. "Got it." Which meant they were halfway, and the worst was over. "Which way at the top?"

"Back," grunted Trevor, making the turn. "Says it will be her office."

"At least this is the biggest piece."

"You haven't seen the bookcases yet, I take it."

Lauren and Denae jogged up the stairs behind them as they set the desk in the middle of the room.

"Right over here." Denae pointed toward the left. "I want to see the mountains while I work."

James hated to be a dream-breaker. "Window's not that low."

Denae crouched, mimicking sitting on a chair, and her face fell. "Oh, no. I was so looking forward to the view."

"You could sleep upstairs and use the downstairs bedroom for the office. The windows are bigger."

"No," James and Trevor said in unison.

"Maybe I could get my landlady up here with a chainsaw to put in a bigger window?" Denae tossed Lauren a saucy grin.

"In your dreams. Look, I know this place isn't ideal. It's much smaller than you're used to. I get that, but there aren't many rentals in town. I only snagged this from my dad's estate so I didn't have to live with my mother anymore."

Doc Yanovich had bought up several rental properties back when the town was half empty and houses were cheap. Lauren's mom, Dora, had sold most of them after her husband died, turning a pretty penny.

"It's fine, Lauren. I was just kidding. Although if you had said it was doable, I wouldn't have complained."

"What are you planning for the other bedroom up here?" James peered down the hall.

"I thought a guest bedroom."

"There's no way anything bigger than a twin box spring will fit up those stairs. Trevor and I are good, but we're not magicians."

Deep in thought, Denae pursed her lips and narrowed her eyes, but James's gaze caught on Lauren's face. She looked super sad, like it was all her fault. He stepped closer and bumped her shoulder with his arm. "Hey."

She leaned away just enough to break contact and looked up at him. "Hey, yourself."

"It'll all work out."

Denae walked down the short hall into the other room, Trevor at her heels. Their low voices filtered back as they discussed whether Denae's plan was possible. A tape measure rattled.

Lauren shook her head. "Sometimes I think I should sell this place and buy something laid out a bit better. Quit having a rental."

His heart ached with all his hopes. "Why don't you?"

"It's so close to the clinic. I thought at first I'd walk to work, but I need my Wrangler for call-outs, so I drive anyway. And... I've been here four years and it doesn't feel like home. I don't get to spend that much time here."

"I'm sorry."

"No need for pity." She pushed off the wall and strode over to the small window overlooking the backyard. "I'm lucky to have all this. To have made it through vet school. To be a partner in the clinic my dad helped start."

He knew that. He remembered how hard she'd studied and planned to meet her goals. She'd always been independent. Driven. He admired that about her, but he wanted to offer her more.

More what? He all but lived with his parents, and she definitely couldn't walk to work from the ranch. "I'm thinking of building a house," he heard himself say.

She turned, arms crossed over her chest, her short dark curls framing her face. "You are?"

That the thought had taken root surprised him, too. "Out on the ranch, of course. Probably timber frame. Dad and I have been looking at building spots." He hesitated, praying his brain would catch up to his mouth. "I haven't picked out a design or anything. The build might not be be until next year. I could use another eye analyzing floor plans."

Lauren pivoted toward the window. "Denae's really good at stuff like that. She took interior design in college before deciding to become an editor."

When would she stop foisting her friends on him? "I asked you."

She shrugged, her back still to him. "I don't have opinions worth hearing."

"I think you do."

"That's sweet of you, James. I'm happy for you. It should be a lot of fun, seeing your home come to reality before your eyes."

Fun? It sounded like a million piddly decisions, probably all coming in a machine gun blast during the busy tourist season. It sounded empty. Lonely. "It will be nice, I think."

"Denae's spare king-size bed will barely fit in the room, never mind up the stairs," announced Trevor. "No room to walk around it. You'd have to jump in from the doorway."

"I don't know what I was thinking." Denae followed Trevor into the back bedroom-slash-office, her cheeks flushed. "I'll have to go shopping for something smaller. Or does the Hats Off Motel have king beds? Maybe Dad and Michelle can rent a room when they're visiting overnight. That won't be very often since it's only a couple of hours from Missoula."

"I have plenty of room," Trevor said. "If you need a place to put up guests, send them my way. Any of you."

Testy Trevor wasn't interested in the scrawny editor, was he? If it went both ways, Lauren would have to stop throwing Denae at James. *Go, Trevor!*

"That might be a solution." Denae beamed at Trevor. "It won't happen often. I promise."

James turned to the hall, hiding a grin. "Okay, so we should figure out what else needs to come up these stairs, then. I heard there would be pizza, and I'm starving."

James is building a house.

Lauren couldn't shake the thought. It meant he'd met someone — obviously not Denae — and was thinking toward the future. Who had caught his eye? She could envision a sprawling log house with a troop of little cowpokes in it out on the gorgeous Flying Horseshoe. A big kitchen, worthy of a ranch house, with alder cabinetry and a massive butcher-block island in a sea of granite counters. A woman stood looking out the expansive sink window, stubbornly refusing to turn and reveal her identity to Lauren.

This was what she wanted for him. To fall in love, get married, and be happy. Right?

It was. But only if the woman was her, and there was no chance of that. James didn't love her. He'd had years to act on it if he did. Yeah, they were good friends, but there was a huge chasm between friends and lovers. If there was a way to bridge that abyss, she hadn't found it.

Lauren had stood staring into the postage-stamp-sized backyard so long that James and Trevor were stuck in the stair landing again, this time with a bookcase. They muttered to each other amid the thuds of wood on carpet.

She couldn't take this any longer. Maybe she should try to sell her half of the business. Sell her duplex. Leave Saddle Springs and her annoying, interfering mother.

Leave James.

Not before their thirtieth birthday, just in case he

came through, but she'd consider it more closely afterward. Her heart warred with itself like a dog chewing its own leg off to escape a trap. She didn't want to be James's best friend or pity project. Not anyone's. She wanted to be loved beyond measure. To be swept off her feet as someone's entire universe. James's sun and moon and stars.

Was it too much to ask? *God?* Staring down the barrel at thirty indicated her dreams had been too big. Too crazy. Too selfish.

One of the men grunted as they lowered the tall bookcase to the floor behind her.

She turned. James wiped sweat from his brow as he grinned at her. "She's lucky to have you for a friend, is all I can say. And that you know how to bribe your other friends."

Yeah, that's all it was. James was a kind-hearted man who always watched out for the underdog. No mean bones in his body.

Trevor laughed and jogged down the stairs.

"Have you come up with a name for the filly yet?"

Lauren shook her head. She'd probably spend less time naming her firstborn. Why this opportunity paralyzed her, she had no idea.

"Tori's threatening to call her Yanni."

She frowned. "Yanni?"

"Short for Yanovich."

"Um, no. Terrible idea."

"My nephew suggested Mud."

"What on earth?"

"Aiden is obsessed with puddles. Thankfully it's starting to dry up out there and the grass is peeking through." James studied her. "You haven't been out for a few days."

It was true. The foal's birth had seemed so intimate she'd stayed away all week. It had almost seemed like something passed between her and James that night but, just like always, time ticked on and nothing changed. Either he was the most clueless guy on the planet, or they really were only friends like they'd both always claimed.

"While I hate to disappoint a three-year-old, I'll come up with something better than Mud. Promise."

His eyes crinkled when he smiled. "I'm counting on it. Although Yanni isn't so bad."

"Funny boy."

James leaned closer. "It's your call, Lauren."

Her knees went weak, and she sagged against the window. Why was he so close? Filling her vision with his gorgeous face, neatly trimmed beard, and intense blue eyes? Filling her senses with his masculine cologne? Her ears with his soft, melodic voice? Although she could barely hear his words over the pounding of her heart.

His hand touched her arm and then he was gone, his feet thudding down the carpeted steps.

Lauren inhaled sharply and rubbed the spot where he'd touched. What was her call? Was he still talking about the filly? Because that was a whole lot of intensity for a newborn horse. Far more fervor than it deserved. Wasn't it?

She pulled herself together and jogged down the

stairs. "Rosebud," she announced, brushing past James in the doorway.

"Rosebud?"

"For the filly. What do you think?"

He lifted a shoulder. "Sure. Works for me."

"Okay, then. I'm off the hook." She looked around the main floor with oversized furniture crowding the space. "How much more to unload?" The answer better be 'nothing' because there was no place to put it.

"A few things for upstairs. Two more bookcases." Denae smiled brightly. "And about twenty boxes of books."

Trevor groaned. "Why so many?"

"I'm an editor," she informed him. "And even before that, I was an avid reader. Consider them my collection."

"I carried in four boxes labeled *figurines: fragile*."

"That's my other collection."

James looked out the open doorway. "Let's get them before it rains. Shouldn't take too long, right?"

Ever the optimist.

"I'll head next door and get the pizza ordered, if you all think half an hour is long enough. What kind do you like?"

James opened his mouth.

"Besides you. It's always double the pepperoni and add jalapeños for you."

He grinned. "You know me so well."

Did she? It wasn't nearly well enough.

Chapter 6

Garret rocked his wooden chair in Java Springs back on two legs and eyed Kade. "So, how's married life treating you?"

Kade offered a lopsided grin and a small shrug. "Definitely can't complain."

James focused on twisting his coffee cup round and round, listening to the ceramic base scraping the table. Being happy for his buddy was hard right now. Kade Delgado had always been one of the good guys. A loyal friend. A listening ear. Steady as the shifting seasons. He'd been jilted, raised his young son alone for over two years, and been reunited with the love of his life. He deserved happiness.

Except it shone a shaft of light on the emptiness in James's life. It'd been a couple of weeks since the day they'd moved Denae in, and he'd only seen Lauren at church since. He'd had no reason to call her to the ranch as a veterinarian, and no other schemes presented themselves. He hadn't needed schemes in the past. Pizza and a movie, a horseback ride, jamming some music... all valid. And now they all sounded forced.

"And the new house?" asked Garret.

James pulled his focus back to the conversation. "Are you happy with Timber Framing Plus? We're thinking of hiring them for more guest cabins."

Kade shot him a sharp look. "That's not what I heard."

"And maybe a house for me." James shook his head. "I'm not sure I want one."

Garret's chair thumped to all fours. "Why not? Man, I'd give anything to spread my wings a little. This working-for-the-parents thing has its perks, but living arrangements isn't one of them."

James forced a chuckle. "Guess I always figured I'd build when I had a wife, and that seems farther off than ever."

Kade's arms crossed over his chest. "Have you told her how you feel?"

"And sound super pathetic when she doesn't feel the same?"

"Maybe she's as good an actor as you are."

"You think?" James straightened. Was it possible?

"You *are* pathetic." Kade shook his head. "Are you seriously just going to keep letting things drift along forever? At some point, you have to man up."

"Easy for you to say."

His friend's eyebrows shot up as he offered a piercing look. "Easy to *say*, maybe, but not easy to *do*. You were there with me and Cheri. You know."

James did know. He sagged back into his chair. "Not forever, no. We'll soon be thirty."

"And that's significant because...?" Garret looked from one to the other.

"Kade knows."

But Kade's brow furrowed. "What're you talking about, man?"

"When we were sixteen. Remember? Dillon had just ditched Lauren, and..."

Light dawned on Kade's face. "And you told her if she was still single at thirty, you'd marry her."

"We high-fived on it." That was practically the same thing as blood vows.

"And that's why you've hardly dated in the last decade? Because you're carrying a torch for Lauren Yanovich and are just waiting for the end of some kind of self-imposed exile?"

"Shh." James glanced around the quiet coffee shop. Thankfully they were the only ones in the space.

"You're kidding, right?" asked Garret. "I know you guys tease me because I'm so gullible."

Kade peered into James's eyes and shook his head slowly. "I don't think we're kidding. Are we, Carmichael?"

"You make it sound so..."

"Woeful? Because it is."

James took a deep breath and pushed his coffee cup

away. He leaned forward on the table. "Look, here's the thing. She's not interested. Okay?"

"Because she's told you?"

"Because it's as clear as the nose on my face. Because she pushes all her friends on me and even women she doesn't actually know, like that new waitress at The Branding Iron. She thinks she's doing me a favor."

"Anna?" asked Garret. "She's hot."

"Is she? I wouldn't know. I haven't put a boot in the door since Lauren told me about her."

"Listen to me." Kade stared into his eyes. "Women are strange creatures, okay? Their decisions often don't make any sense to guys. Trust me on this. Cheri vanished for years because she didn't think she could talk to me, and we weren't casual acquaintances. We were about to be married. In a week."

James nodded. He'd marveled when the whole story had tumbled out. What had Cheri been thinking? But, more to the point — for him, anyway — what was Lauren thinking?

"So, what do we need to do to help you along?" Garret's eyes livened with interest. "She needs to see what a great deal she's trying to pawn off on a friend."

"Nothing." James sliced his hand through the air. "Don't do anything. You can pray for me. Not that it will help, but whatever."

"Need a refill, boys?" Abigail Evening stood at the end of the table, coffee pot in hand. "And another batch of peach muffins just came out of the oven. Your favorite, James." She smiled brightly at him.

What had she overheard? Anything?

Garret pushed his cup down the table and patted his belly. "A muffin sounds great."

James nodded and gulped the last of his cold coffee before extending his cup.

"I've got to go. I promised Cheri I'd pick up her list from Manahan's and be home early."

Abigail beamed at Kade. "And those sweet children need their daddy. Let me send a few muffins. Tell Cheri to stop by next time she's in town."

He chuckled. "More like my sweet wife has eighty decisions we need to make on the new house before next week. Who knew there were dozens of cabinetry styles, each available in ten kinds of hardwood with five hundred hardware options and who-knows-how-many countertops? And that's only the kitchen."

Abigail laughed. "Don't forget appliances and floors."

Kade pushed out of his chair as she poured for James and Garret. "Think how much easier it will be to build a house by yourself, man. Lay out all the options, close your eyes, and point. Done. Move onto the next decision."

"Just make Cheri do all the picking," suggested Garret. "Why get involved at all?"

"That's not how it works." Kade's laugh lines showed around his eyes. "I promise, when you have a gorgeous wife like I do, you want to keep her happy. Really happy, if you get my drift."

"Get out of here and take your innuendoes with you." James made a shooing motion. "Sheesh. Me 'n Garret don't need you putting those thoughts in our virtuous heads."

Kade chuckled as he plunked his cowboy hat on his head and strode for the door, whistling.

Whistling.

James couldn't remember the last time he'd felt like whistling. Everything inside him was so tied up in knots he could barely get through each day.

Abigail slid a plate of muffins on the table and admonished them to holler if they needed anything else.

"Mmm, good," mumbled Garret around a full mouth.

"Yeah." James reached for a muffin and slathered some butter on it as Abigail headed for the kitchen.

"So, is it true?"

"Is what true?"

"That you made a pledge with Lauren when you were kids."

"Teens. But yes."

"That's amazing. I bet she thinks you've forgotten all about it."

"You've got your britches on backwards." James laughed. "She's the one who's forgotten, not me."

"Delgado's got a point, though. You don't know that."

"It doesn't matter. I'll figure something out." He needed a change of subject. Stat. "Hey, did Tori talk to you about her trail ride camping trip idea? You in?"

"She did. I am *so* in. Who else is going?"

"Lauren and Denae."

Garret's eyebrows lifted.

"Don't even think it. Tori's running the show. She invited Kade and Cheri, too, but they can't get away. Same with Carmen. She asked a few other people, but it looks like just the five of us. Thanks for making me be not the only guy."

"It could be worse."

"Oh?"

"It could be all guys with no women to do the cooking."

"I'm a decent hand at campfire cooking. It's a skill every man should have."

Garret snagged a second muffin and inhaled it in three bites before rising. "I like my ignorance, thanks. I'll be the one sitting by the campfire playing the flute while everyone else works."

He probably would be, too.

***

Lauren nudged Luna into a canter as Tori, mounted on Coaldust, led the way around the lake on the Flying Horseshoe. She hadn't been riding in much too long and hadn't been able to resist Tori's invitation. Besides, she needed to get her muscles back in shape for next month's long trail ride.

Behind her, Denae whooped as Pippi Longstocking put on a matching burst of speed.

Tori grinned over her shoulder.

Now that girl looked like she was part of her mount.

But then, she'd been raised on the place and probably rode every day. Lauren had to wait for an invite to one of her friends' ranches. Garret's family stabled horses for other townspeople, though. She should look into buying her own horse and boarding it at Canyon Crossing.

She leaned forward and ran her hand over Luna's black mane. Pretty sweet mare and likely very popular with guests. It wasn't likely the Carmichaels would ever part with her.

James would say Lauren was welcome to come ride Luna any time. She knew that, but it meant seeing James. Although, today she'd managed to escape the ranch yard with Tori and Denae without running into him. She should feel more relief at that. The guy twisted her in knots. Something had to give, and soon.

When they trotted into a clearing on the far side of the lake, Lauren reined in and took in the view. The lake wasn't all that big, but large enough for swimming, fishing, and paddling. The gang had met here all through their teen years. So many good memories.

Back across the lake, the row of guest cabins marched along the shore, shielded from the ranch house by a row of trees. The corrals and stables lay closer to Creighton Road.

She took a deep breath, inhaling the pine-scented air, fragrant with the new growth of early spring. Red-winged blackbirds trilled in the rushes at water's edge. The mountain stream that fed the lake tumbled in just ahead, a sturdy log bridge offering safe crossing over the slippery rocks.

The Flying Horseshoe was as close to heaven as possible on this planet.

"...over here."

Lauren blinked back into the moment and nudged Luna up a small rise to where Tori gestured to Denae.

"What are you talking about?"

"Where James is going to build. Creighton Road curves near here, which Dad says is important for utilities. Plus, it's not far from Meg's place."

The middle Carmichael sibling had married last year and lived in the ranch's secondary house with her small family. Meg had always been the wild one. Amazing she'd been able to snag a man as solid as Eli Thornton when she had a little kid in tow.

Not that Lauren had anything against young Aiden. The sweetheart was in her Sunday school class along with Kade's little guy, Jericho, and a host of others. Someday she wanted—

No. She pulled her attention back to Tori and trotted Luna around the knoll and up the slight incline to the clearing. The view was even better from up here. Trees blocked most of the main ranch on the east side but left half the lake, while the drop-off to the west insured a view of a glacier high in the mountains.

Pegs had been hammered into the ground with a spray of paint connecting them. And James said he hadn't picked a layout yet? That had been a week ago. Obviously, she was behind the times. Her heart tightened a little more.

"This is amazing." Denae turned her mount in a

circle as she scanned the views. "A house up here with a view like this? Total chick magnet."

Tori giggled. "Now that's good news. I've despaired of anything making him attractive enough to finally get himself a girl."

"Brothers. I know how it is."

Lauren didn't. But there was nothing wrong with James's magnetism. How could they even think that? "Although he's not so bad even without the house. A voice like his? His guitar pickin' skills?"

Tori laughed. "A guy can't sing and dance his way through life like in the musicals, and you still have to look at his ugly mug."

"He's not ugly!" Lauren couldn't help the words.

His sister shrugged and turned away. "I call 'em like I see 'em. I could be biased against his looks."

Denae giggled. "I think he's cute. Right, Lauren?"

A flush crept up Lauren's cheeks. "At least he's a long way from ugly." A really, really long way.

"Right. You guys have been best friends forever," Tori tossed over her shoulder. "I guess you'd have steered clear if he were that horrid."

"Best friends, huh?" Denae's eyes gleamed.

"Don't get any ideas." Lauren forced a chuckle. "A bunch of us have known each other since we were kids and never got over hanging out together. It definitely wasn't just him and me." She pointed back across the creek at the ring of rocks closer to the water's edge, where a few lengths of charcoal showed through tufts of grass. "We all used to come out here, talk and sing around the bonfire until the wee hours. Didn't you join us a few times in the summers you stayed with your dad?"

Denae sighed. "I visited a lot when I was a kid, but by the time I was fifteen, I mostly lived with my mom. I had a summer job and friends in Cannon Beach. My dad didn't push hard for me."

"What happened to change that?" Tori circled Coaldust around to face them.

"I couldn't believe it when Dad and Michelle sold Standing Rock to the Delgados. He didn't even tell me ahead of time, just did it, as if them moving to Missoula wouldn't even matter to me. I guess he had no way of knowing..."

"Guys are terrible at mind-reading," agreed Tori. "Never changes. Mom complains about that with Dad all the time. She figures something is obvious, but he's totally oblivious."

Was that really a thing?

"Yeah. My stepdad and little brothers, too. You have to spell everything out to them in words of one syllable. While making eye contact."

This sounded like male-bashing. But what if it were true? What if James had no clue how Lauren really felt because he couldn't read her mind? On top of that, she sent mixed signals. She knew she did. She'd put herself forward a little and, when he didn't immediately respond in the perfect way, she backpedaled so he'd never have a chance.

What was she supposed to do? Grab a fistful of his

snap-front shirt, look up at him, and tell him she'd loved him forever? Beg him to kiss her?

Then she'd see either hilarity or horror spread across his gorgeous face.

She couldn't take the risk.

Chapter 7

James strummed his guitar as Garret's fingers flew over the keyboard nearby. This morning it was only the two of them leading worship… the new normal with how often Lauren had begged off in the past few months.

Garret nodded at him, leaned into his microphone, and began to sing. James's voice melded from the first word of the old hymn, and he kept an eye on his friend. Garret was known for varying the timing.

Be Thou my vision, O lord of my heart. Naught be all else to me, save that Thou art — Thou my best thought by day or by night...

James focused on the words, like he should have been focusing on God these past few months rather than on Lauren. Human love was great, or so he assumed, but he'd gotten his priorities whacked off course lately. The words and music heightened to a crescendo.

Be Thou my wisdom, and Thou my true word, I ever with

Thee, and Thou with me, Lord. Thou my great Father, and I Thy true son...

His heart lifted within him at the thought. How had he become so nearsighted? So trusting in his own wisdom?

Heart of my own heart, whatever befall, still be my vision, O ruler of all...

Incomprehensible. To think of being so united with God that their hearts beat as one, of finding all his treasure in the High King of Heaven. Yet... comforting. He was too full of himself. Too focused on little Jamie Carmichael's wishes and dreams.

The song came to an end and Pastor Roland approached the platform. James lifted the guitar strap over his head and set his instrument into its stand at the back of the platform before following Garret down the four steps. They slipped into their seats on the side aisle, second row. Far from where Lauren sat toward the back with Denae. Yeah, he'd noticed. Sue him.

"Does God have one perfect will for your life?" asked the pastor.

This should be good. James hunkered down in the pew and gave over his full attention.

Well, duh. Of course, the answer was yes.

Lauren crossed her arms and stared at Pastor Roland. Who didn't want God's perfect will for her life? Or his, as the case might be? To even suggest otherwise was nothing less than heresy.

"There are several questions linked with that one. Is there one house and one job that God has earmarked for you? Is there one perfect person for you to marry?"

Yes, yes, and yes. She might have messed up on the perfect house, but she had her perfect job. The perfect spouse seemed a tad out of reach at the moment, but she had faith. Faith that God would either grant her prayer... or get her ridiculous infatuation with James Carmichael out of her head when He brought her perfect match to her.

Removing her love for James would require a lot of erasing, though. But God was big. Powerful. He could do it, even if He had to douse her with full amnesia to accomplish it.

She didn't want to forget everything. She wanted it to come true. It wasn't going to, though. Time was ticking, and James was no closer to falling in love with her than he'd ever been.

"Those questions are linked to fate, and they can cause a lot of stress. Imagine being seventeen again." Pastor Roland cracked a grin.

Lauren would rather not go there.

"A high school senior is faced with a lot of decisions. Some of you are in that boat right now. Which college should you go to? What should you study? Maybe you should go to trade school or work a year first. To compound it, everyone around you has an opinion. Ask my son Matt."

"Don't!" yelled a teenage guy from up a few rows.

Lauren couldn't help grinning as everyone laughed.

"That's right. Matt's tired of the questions. He feels enough pressure inside himself that he doesn't need advice from those not invested in his life. So, let's break this down a bit, shall we?"

"Your pastor is a bit odd," whispered Denae.

Normally Lauren would step up in defense but, at the moment, she had to agree. She had a funny feeling she wasn't going to like this sermon.

"Is it wrong to want to do God's will? Not at all. If we didn't, we'd have to question our love for Him. The Bible is a book for the ages. We can search it for God's will, and we'll find verses that are very helpful."

A reference flashed up onto the screen.

"First Thessalonians four verse three says, 'It is God's will that you should be sanctified; that you should avoid sexual immorality.' So that's very clear, and helpful for all of us."

The screen changed.

"Likewise, First Timothy two, verses three through four say, 'this is good and pleases God our Savior, who wants all people to be saved and to come to a knowledge of the truth.' So, we know God's will is for everyone to understand the truth.

"Paul, in Ephesians five, lists several things as direct orders: 'be careful how you live, make the most of every opportunity, don't be foolish, do not get drunk on wine, be filled with the Spirit, and give thanks to God the Father for everything.' In Micah six, verse eight, we see that God has shown us what is good. 'What does the Lord require of you? To act justly and to love mercy and to walk humbly with your God.'"

Pastor Roland leaned on the podium and looked around the sanctuary. "Anyone see anything in the scripture that says, 'Matt, you should attend Montana State, study engineering, move to Helena and take a career with X Company, buy a house on Meadow Drive, and marry the first woman you meet at the coffee shop on the corner'?"

Matt groaned into the silence following his dad's question. A few people chuckled.

"It's not in there, is it? You're off the hook, Matt. Greenwood Street is as good as Meadow. No problem."

Pastor Roland sipped his water. "Do you think that if Matt goes to U of M instead of Montana State, he's sinning? That he's so off-course from God's will that he can't get back on it for the rest of his life? That God has no backup plan? Imagine if Matt never enters that coffee shop on the corner. Will he miss out on the perfect woman God has for him? Is God's will for his life that narrow?"

Fabric rustled and pews squeaked as people shifted in their seats.

"We all face decisions every day. Sometimes when we look back, we can see how a small choice resulted in big changes. You might get out to the car having forgotten your library books, dash back in for them, and proceed into town to discover an accident has taken place two minutes before, right where you would have been had you remembered the books in the first place. You might linger over coffee with friends at Java Springs long enough to be present when someone you've lost touch with enters."

He had to be talking about Cheri and Kade there. But it was a reasonable question. What if Kade had left the coffee shop five minutes earlier? His life story with Cheri might have taken a different spin. Or if there hadn't been a blizzard that night. Or... so many things. That had to mean God had orchestrated their Christmas reunion from above, right?

"If we don't find God's express will for each individual in the Bible, does that mean our choices aren't important? Again, not so. We have plenty of instructions in God's word about how to live and make decisions. The book of James instructs us, 'if any of you lacks wisdom, you should ask God, who gives generously to all without finding fault, and it will be given to you.'"

The dude James in the Bible was a super practical sort, not so different from James the cowboy. She knew rancher James loved God, depended on Him, likely asked for wisdom. Did he pray for her? About her? What would God tell him if he did?

What was God telling her?

"There are other scriptures about what God's will is. I want to challenge each of you to do a personal search this week or get together with your spouse or friends and dig into your concordance. Or, you know, Google it. Pop into the church's Facebook group and add the verses you find to the thread I'll pin this afternoon. Let's challenge each other to find out what God's will is directly from His word, and not from our assumptions and long-held beliefs. Let's pray."

After Pastor Roland's prayer, James and Garret returned to the platform and struck up the opening chords to John Waller's *While I'm Waiting.*

Was she doing anything useful while she waited? Was she serving? Worshiping? Or was she doing everything she could to take things into her own hands and influence the outcome? What would happen if she simply asked God for wisdom while seeking His will boldly and confidently?

SUNDAY LUNCH at the Flying Horseshoe could be labeled family dinner. Meg, Eli, and Aiden might cruise through a time or two during the week, but Sunday after church wasn't optional for any of them.

Today, James wished it was. He'd rather take Jigsaw out for a run and think about Pastor Roland's sermon with the wind on his face. Instead, as always, it would be a family dissection.

Meg and Tori were already into it in the kitchen when he strolled in.

"I think he meant there's no single perfect path for anyone." Meg's tone indicated this might be a repeat. "Which totally makes sense. I'm not the only person who ever screwed up with bad decisions."

"And then turned her life around," Mom put in. Pans clanked in the kitchen.

"But wouldn't it have been better if you hadn't made a mess?" Tori insisted.

"God gives second chances. I don't think of Aiden or Eli as second best."

Yikes. This wasn't a conversation in which James wished to participate. He veered toward the family room where his nephew had just dumped out a heap of bright-colored plastic building blocks leftover from years gone by. James dropped beside the mound. "Hey, Aiden."

"Unca James! How you?"

"Good, buddy. Did you go to Sunday school today?"

"Wi' Miss Lauren."

Right. He should have remembered where that would lead him. Where all pathways in his mind led: Lauren. "Did you learn about Jesus today?"

"Yeah. 'Bout He died."

Lauren did a good job with the little ones. "He did die. Did she tell you the rest?"

"He alive again. He lub me."

"You got it in one, buddy." Easter had been a few weeks back. Pastor Roland might have moved on to different sermon topics, but apparently the kids' curriculum was still on the subject. Probably just as well. Today's discourse would be hard to bring down to a three-year-old level. Or maybe not. God's will for little kids was simple and pure: obeying their parents, being kind and thankful... what else?

His brother-in-law lowered himself beside Aiden. "How tall a tower can you build? Bigger than Uncle James?"

James glanced at Eli and caught the grin. "Aiden might be able to, but can *you*?"

"Oh, a challenge! You're on."

Dad chuckled from his recliner near the fireplace. "Is that God's will for you boys?"

James fitted several blocks together to form a solid base. "Think He cares one way or the other?"

"The results might prove which one of us God loves best," Eli teased.

"Yeah, totally. I can see that. It's probably you. You're practically a saint for loving my sister."

Eli began stacking blocks. "But I don't have a book of the Bible named after me."

"No, but your biblical alter-ego was a pretty good guy. Followed God."

"Also, he had lazy, rebellious sons."

"Aiden will never be rebellious, will you, buddy?" James ruffled the little guy's hair.

Aiden grabbed James's tower and removed the red blocks from the top.

James tugged it back, capping it with blue ones. "Hey, are you trying to make me lose?"

"Good job, Aiden." Eli worked faster.

"Now you're cheating, dude. Not only that, you're teaching your kid that the end justifies the means."

"Am I?" Eli asked blandly. "God's will for dads is not to exasperate their children. Says so in the Bible. That'd be Ephesians."

"There's more to it." James reached for the yellow blocks Eli had pulled to the side, elbowing his brother-in-law's tower in the process and knocking it in pieces. "Oops."

"Some accident there, dude." Eli dusted his hands together, and James's tower tumbled. "You're right, there's more. Also supposed to bring him up in the training and instruction of the Lord."

"And possibly be a good example of treating your brother with kindness and respect?" James swept a circle through the scattered blocks, gathering them to his side.

"Playing fair." Eli scooped the blocks back. "A good skill to learn."

Aiden danced in the cleared spot.

James leaned back on his hands and laughed.

"People are already commenting on Roland's sermon on Facebook." Dad waved his phone. "Gloria Delgado added one of my favorites. Proverbs three, verse five. 'Trust in the Lord with all your heart and lean not on your own understanding.' I'm going to like her comment, because she's right. That's a clear indication of what God wants us to do." He focused hard and poked at the phone with one big finger.

James exchanged a grin with Eli. "I'll check the group later and see if I think of anything to add." Likely he'd do the same as his father. Like a bunch of comments and carry on with his week.

It was going to be another busy one.

Chapter 8

"That house James is planning to build is going to be suh-weet."

Lauren jerked her head upright and stared at Denae. Since when was her friend hanging out with James after hours? *Relax. Relax. Don't bite her head off. You've been pushing her his direction, after all.*

Yeah, but that didn't mean she actually wanted it to come true.

"I ran into him and the guy from Timber Framing Plus at Java Springs this afternoon going over floor plans. James wanted a woman's opinion on a few things." Denae dropped into the chair across Lauren's tiny kitchen table, forked her fingers into her long black hair at the temples, and began French braiding it.

"Oh? Like what?" Lauren could do this. Maintain nonchalance. Be happy for James and Denae.

"There were a few options, like whether to have the interior walls made all of wood or drywalled." Denae shuddered. "Imagine that much wood, plus on the cabinets and floors. Men. Don't they know a bit of variety and color never hurt anyone?"

Wood suited James. It was raw, natural. Of course, he'd go for that look. "So, you told him drywall?"

"Definitely." Denae slid the elastic from her wrist and tied the end of her braid. "Not sure I convinced him, though."

Lauren managed a smile. "I imagine he'll make his own decision." That he'd asked Denae at all grated.

"The contractor, Brent Callahan, offered pros and cons both ways, so I'm not sure what James will choose. Brent has been building houses for six or seven years now and worked for his uncle before that. He has quite a bit of experience. He's cute." Denae sighed. "But married."

"There are plenty of unmarried cute men right here in Saddle Springs. Cowboys have to beat contractors any day of the week. What's not to love about jeans and cowboy hats?"

"I know, right? And some of the ranchers around here have plenty of money."

Not all of them. Lauren knew a few who struggled to pay their veterinary bills.

"James said he wanted to build a small house," Denae went on. "His parents reminded him he'd have a family one day, and he'd wish he'd built a bigger one."

Visions of little Carmichaels with their daddy's dark hair and bright blue eyes darted through Lauren's mind. James was so hands-on with his nephew, she could imagine him with half a dozen of his own. She looked at

Denae more closely. Would dark brown eyes dominate over blue? "So, who's winning?"

"I think they're compromising. He's going with two bedrooms down and two up, but it's fairly compact at under two thousand square feet on the main floor."

Compared to the duplex, that was palatial. Not that Lauren was jealous. Much. It wasn't the space so much as the location and the vistas. And the man, if she forced herself to face it.

Why couldn't she just invite James out for a ride and tell him how she really felt? Put everything out there once and for all?

No way. Not after Conor back at MSU. He'd thought she should be happy as a veterinary assistant and didn't need more schooling. He'd thought she should live far from her intrusive mother. Well, she couldn't quite fault the guy for that one but, in reality, she hadn't quite matched Conor's expectations. He had a specific slot for "future wife" — good education, but not more than him. Pretty... and one who didn't stress-eat during exam week then wear sweats to hide the extra pounds. The perfect cook and hostess, while still holding down the job that would help maintain the household. Doubtless Conor's children would all be scrubbed behind the ears, well-mannered, and never rip holes in the knees of their jeans. If they were allowed jeans, that is.

Point was, Lauren had tried to be the woman Conor wanted, only to discover he'd never be satisfied. He hadn't even bothered with the *it's not you, it's me* bit. No, he'd put it all on her. Her unreasonable expectations for what was obviously beyond her, even with the coveted acceptance letter to veterinary college in hand. He felt sorry for her, for the sure disappointments to follow, but he wouldn't be there for any of them. He was done.

And then she'd overheard him with his buddies on campus, laughing over her unreasonable expectations. Who did she think she was, choosing stinky barns over dating an architect with a partnership in his dad's esteemed company? Her inheritance wasn't worth it. She wasn't that cute, anyway. And not interested in going to the gym to get rid of that extra fat. Conor was humiliated. Whew — he'd had a lucky escape.

Her ears had burned as she scurried away. And she'd redoubled her efforts to be enough in herself, since Conor was right — no real man would want her. Good thing she didn't need one.

"Lauren?"

She blinked at Denae. "Um... sorry? I was lost there for a minute. What did you say?"

Denae grinned. "James asked why you and I didn't come out and have a look at the building site. I told him we already had."

Play it cool. "He invited *me*? I didn't know he was the kind of guy who couldn't make decisions without a group-think."

"Aw, come on. You've known him forever, haven't you?" Denae leaned back in her chair, shaking her head. "I really wish I'd stuck with my dad as a teen. Think what I missed with all these hunky cowboys. They were just scrawny kids last time I knew them. And now Kade's already taken, but there's Trevor or James or that new guy, Garret." She sighed. "Who would you pick?"

Lauren stared at her friend sitting there with her eyes closed and a dreamy smile lifting her lips. "Who would I *pick*?"

Denae opened her eyes. "Yes. That's what I asked."

"I wouldn't pick any of them." Lauren surged to her feet and poured herself an iced tea from the pitcher in the fridge. "Want some?"

"Sure. What are you looking for, then? Though I can't see why you'd pass up one of these cowboys. Trevor is to-die-for cute, but he's kind of grumpy. James isn't quite as adorable, but he's more easygoing. And Garret..."

"He's pretty nice."

"I'm not sure about Garret. I mean, he seems cool, but maybe too young for me. But, wow, is he talented. Imagine having a husband who serenaded you with his gorgeous voice while playing the piano."

Lauren had imagined it many a time, at least if the man were James and the instrument a guitar. "Trevor and James both have great voices, too. Trevor and Kade even used to sing duets in church when they were kids."

"Trevor sings?" Denae straightened, eyes wide. "In public? I wouldn't have guessed."

He hadn't, not for a few years. What had changed? Lauren didn't know. She hadn't really thought about it. The oldest Delgado brother had never been on her radar. No, her heart had been completely filled with James Carmichael for nearly fourteen years. She'd tried to get her mind off him with Conor, but it hadn't worked.

"He sings bass. But James... didn't you hear him Sunday? He has an amazing tenor." Lauren forced a grin as she leaned back against the sink cabinet. She needed to get Denae back to James. "And he plays anything with strings. You've got to admit guitars and banjos and ukuleles are more portable than pianos."

So many campfire memories. If only she'd managed to snag James back when they were teens, before she became his pity project. She'd had enough of that from Conor. The only problem was, did James even remember? Because that would make all the difference.

James rolled a fresh tan color over the living room walls in Cabin Two. Every spring they freshened up one or two of the guest cabins, casting a critical eye on all the decorating choices. His sister had decided to go with an Old West theme this time around.

"What color are you going to paint the walls in your new house?" Tori bit her bottom lip as she cut in around the glass doors that led to the deck overlooking the lake.

"One of the options is square log interior walls." James reloaded his roller. "That seems easier than choosing and maintaining colors."

"You're kidding me, right?"

"Uh... no?"

She rolled her eyes. "You're such a guy."

"I hate to break it to you..."

"I know, I know. But, seriously, James. Unless you're

going with painted cabinetry and carpet or tiles on the floor, that's a dumb idea."

His sister sounded like Denae. "I happen to like wood. The hickory cabinets look good with wrought iron handles." He shot her a glance. "I was thinking horseshoe shaped."

She pivoted, a smear of tan paint hitting the glass. "No."

James laughed. "Clean up your mess, girl."

"Clean up your decorating skills," she muttered, grabbing a rag. "Seriously. You need a woman."

He wanted one, too. At least, if her name was Lauren Yanovich, but she was back to avoiding him as though he harbored a den of rattlers.

"I think I'll get the girls together and stage an intervention."

"Sounds fun," he replied blandly. "Just remember who gets the final say. Someone who'll live there." Lauren.

"If you were dating someone, I'd have a better idea whom to send over."

"If I were dating someone, you wouldn't feel the need."

"True."

They worked in blissful silence for a few minutes. It wouldn't last, but he'd take it while he had it.

"So, why don't you date?"

To say it was because he hadn't met the right woman yet would be lying. James generally tried to avoid that where possible. He poured more paint into the tray and reloaded his roller.

Tori paused, brush in the air, watching him.

He glared back. "What? Do I have a smear on my face?"

"I can't figure out why you haven't been out in so long I can't even remember when or who it was."

James shrugged as he tackled the last wall in the room. "We're taking this color around into the eating nook, right?"

"Yes. And you're avoiding me."

"It's just not the right time."

"The right time?"

He could hear the disbelief in his sister's voice. He didn't need to see her face. "Yep. That's what I said. Did the new bedding come in for this place?"

"James."

"Victoria." He mimicked the tone in her voice. "I could ask the same questions of you." He waited a beat. "Notice I'm not doing that. You know why? Because it's none of my business. Just like my dating or lack thereof is none of yours."

"You're so annoying," she muttered.

He bit his tongue instead of throwing the taunt back at her. One of them had to be the grownup here.

"You know what I wish?" she asked after a few minutes.

"Hmm?"

"I wish we were closer. I wish you felt like I was a safe person to talk to. If I've ever blabbed a secret and broken your trust, I don't remember doing so. I've never been all that close to Megan, even though she's a girl and closer to my age. She always had that rebellious, sneaky streak, and now that she seems to be a nice, mature person, she's married and expecting her second kid. Now everything is all about Eli and Aiden."

Let her talk. If Tori was griping about their sister, he was off the hook, at least temporarily.

"I mean, I know that's how she should be, focused on her husband and son, to say nothing of the coming baby. But somehow, I missed my window of opportunity to really be friends with her, you know?"

James murmured an agreement. Tori wasn't wrong about Megan. She'd always been a wild one, never toed the line. Their parents could probably blame most of their gray hair on their middle child.

"But, you."

Drat, Tori was back around. He rolled paint and braced himself.

"We're a lot more alike in personality, and you're only four years older. That's not so much, especially now that we're both adults. I've tried so hard to prove myself. I work hard, I don't gossip, and I think I'm a generally nice person."

Oh, man. "You are. You're great." He glanced over at her.

His sister stared back, a slight frown furrowing her brow. "Then what am I doing wrong? You can tell me."

James shook his head. "It's not you. Honestly. It's me."

"That doesn't cut it, big brother. That's like a horribly cliché breakup line."

"I didn't mean it that way." He stood back and surveyed the room. It looked a lot different than the pastel blue it had been for the past few years. Warmer. More inviting. Not too feminine but, since his sister had chosen it, not too masculine, either. "Nice choice, Tori. You've got a good eye. I might use this shade in my house."

"You're really not going to talk to me, are you?"

His turn to frown. He turned to her. "What do you mean? I'm talking to you right now."

"About paint colors. Not about anything important."

She had the grit and determination of a rookie bronc rider. Unseated, but still in the saddle. He had to admire the quality... which didn't mean he was ready to spill his guts. "How about you? Met any cowboy worth riding into the sunset with?"

Tori curled her lip at him. "Why would I tell you if I did? We don't seem to be friends."

"Oh, come on, sis."

"No. Friendship works both ways. If you won't talk to me, then I've got nothing to say to you." She picked up the paint tray, carried it through the archway into the eating nook, and set it on the drop-cloth-covered table before surveying the space.

Women. Why did they have to be so extreme? James wanted her off his back, but not angry with him. Why couldn't they just hang out? Work together? Chill? He looked over the section he'd just completed — no streaks or bubbles — then followed her into the adjoining space. "Tori, you don't have to take it personally."

"Uh huh." She didn't look at him. "You asked about the bedding. I checked tracking this morning and it's en route. Should be here tomorrow."

"Good news." James clenched his teeth. No wonder he was such a failure with Lauren. He couldn't even carry on a civilized conversation with his own sister, let alone the woman he loved.

CHAPTER 9

Lauren knew better, but somehow her finger hit the signal light lever while her foot tapped the brake of her Wrangler. She was only stopping to check Rosebud since she was passing by. That's all. Truthfully, it was no more than she'd do if the foal had been born at Canyon Crossing or Eaglecrest.

Before she could change her mind, the cowboy striding across the yard glanced over and lifted his hand in greeting. At his heels, Brody gave one bark and wagged his tail.

Her heart stuttered. Why was she doing this to herself? Why poke at her emotions to see if they were still sensitive? They were, okay? Enough. Still, she turned into the Flying Horseshoe's drive and parked beside the stable.

James opened the Jeep's door and leaned over the opening, peering at her. "Hey, Lauren. Everything okay?"

He was so close, oozing the comforting scents of horses and oiled leather. His denim shirt stretched over his torso, the snaps pulling with his arm resting above the door opening. His blue eyes looked guarded, like he expected bad news.

"Hi there. I was just driving by on my way back from Sutherlands' place and thought I'd stop in and see how Rosebud is doing. She's what, two weeks old now?"

"Twenty days."

Why didn't he budge? She couldn't very well exit the Jeep while he blocked her way. For an instant she imagined stepping into his space and wrapping her arms around him. Feeling his arms cradle her. Yeah. That would never happen. He'd had over a decade to make his move and was unlikely to suddenly come to his senses. Unless he remembered and was biding his time, but she'd seen no indication of that. She'd notice.

"So, Snowball and Rosebud are doing well? I've got a few minutes and would love to have a look." It wasn't until she unbuckled and swung her leg out that James shifted a few steps out of her way. So much for her snatch of daydream.

He shoved both hands in his jeans pockets and poked his chin toward the maze of runs and corrals beyond the stables. "They're out getting some fresh air. You can see for yourself."

"It's lovely and warm this morning." Lauren fell into step beside him, keeping the dog between them. "You guys ready for the tourist season?"

"Getting there. Tori and I painted Cabin Two earlier this week. Eli replaced a set of taps that proved to be leaking when we turned the water back on in Cabin

Four." He leaned against the split-log corral fence and pointed toward the mare and her foal.

Lauren watched a moment as Rosebud suckled, her tail swishing. The peaceful scene settled over Lauren like a downy blanket. "She's beautiful."

"She's got good lines. If you want a closer look, hop on in."

"No, it's okay. Unless you have concerns." He'd have called the clinic if he did.

James shook his head. "Keeping busy?"

"Always." She forced a chuckle. Did it sound as carefree as she hoped? "Lots of births this time of year. One of Carmen's Border collies has whelped and the other will soon. Meg said something about wanting a puppy for Aiden. I'm sure she and Carmen have been in touch."

"Probably."

Silence stretched for a long moment. Lauren kept her eyes on the mare and foal while every cell in her body yearned to sidle closer to the cowboy beside her. "Do you ever sell riding stock?"

He shifted beside her, brushing her arm. "Not often, unless a horse seems too high-strung for beginning riders. It's rare we don't spot that tendency before we buy, though. Take Coaldust, for instance. He's got a head on him, but Tori's more than capable. That leaves the horse she worked with last year open for guests. Luna."

"I rode her a couple of weeks ago. Good gait."

James nodded. "Looking to buy a horse?"

"Might be. I was thinking of boarding one at Canyon Crossing Stables."

"You can come ride one of ours anytime, you know. No need to be a stranger."

And see James with his look-but-no-touch attitude? There was only so much self-flagellation she could submit herself to. "Morrisons' stables are closer to town."

He scoffed lightly. "By five minutes. Unless you're angling after Garret...?"

Lauren pushed away from the fence and stumbled over Brody, who'd sprawled behind them. The dog rolled out of the way, and James caught her arm before she hit the dust.

"Did I hit a nerve with that one?" he asked.

"Are you kidding me?" Lauren's hands found her hips as she shook off his touch. "You think I'm interested in Garret Morrison?"

He shrugged, not quite meeting her eyes. "Why not? He's a good guy. Can't do much better."

"Who says I'm looking?"

"As you keep telling me, you're pushing thirty."

"That doesn't mean I'm hunting for a husband." If only she could meet his gaze and tell him he was the only man she'd ever wanted.

James tipped his head back and laughed.

It should have warmed her heart, but it had the opposite effect. Did he really care so little about her and her feelings, even after the friendship they'd shared since they were kids? He'd once felt something toward her. Loyalty, at least. Protectionism.

"Turnabout is fair play, Lauren."

She narrowed her eyes and studied him. "I don't know what you're talking about."

"You keep trying to foist your friends off on me but, wow, do you get defensive when the boot's on the other foot." He quirked a brow and met her gaze.

No amusement softened his expression. She chuckled. "It's not the same thing."

"You don't think so?" James leaned back against the fence, hooking his elbows over the railing while one booted heel rested on the bottom board. "I think it is. I'll trust you to make your own decisions if you'll trust me."

Lauren stared at him, a thousand thoughts stampeding through her mind. What would he do if she threw herself at him and told him she loved him? Would he be like Conor, parroting the words back but not meaning them? Letting her down gently — or not so gently — later?

Too much risk. She turned away. "Sure, whatever."

"What does that even mean?"

"It means, fine, I give up. Be old and grumpy and single for all I care. I was just trying to help." She stomped over to the Wrangler and jerked open the driver's door. Why didn't he stop her? If he loved her, he would. She'd been deluding herself all this time, hoping he'd come around. Maybe she *would* date Garret. It would serve James right.

The orange Wrangler burned out of the ranch yard, spinning gravel. The tires squealed a little when they connected with blacktop on the main road.

James stared after it. Took off his Stetson and scratched his head. Yeah, okay. He'd goaded her. He didn't know what kind of reaction he'd expected, but this definitely wasn't it. Who knew people-pleasing Lauren Yanovich had such a temper?

The quiet purr of the guest ranch's golf cart stopped beside him. How much had Dad witnessed? Probably not much. The rev of Lauren's motor had already faded to nothing.

James shoved his hat back on his head and turned to his father. "Hey there."

"Hello, son. What was that all about?"

"Lauren stopped by to check on the foal and now she's headed back to the clinic." Or so he assumed.

"She seemed skittish as an unbroke colt."

"Yeah. Not sure what goes on in a woman's mind." James laughed.

"Sure it was Rosebud she came to see?"

James's gaze caught on his father's angled eyebrows. "Uh. Yes? That's what she said. Why would she lie?"

"Women are confounding creatures. Hard to understand."

"Try telling me something I don't know. Give me a horse any day."

"It's worth the effort, though." Dad went on as though James hadn't spoken. "God made men and women to complement each other. To complete each other."

James pushed out a laugh. "We had the birds-and-the-bees talk years ago, Dad. I haven't forgotten." Sometimes he wished he could. He yearned for Lauren in ways that made him crazy.

"It's more than physical." Dad nudged back his cowboy hat and leaned both elbows on the cart's steering wheel.

"Right. Why are we having this talk?"

"How long are you going to wait? I thought maybe planning your house would remind you, but it hasn't seemed to."

"Wait for what?" The words came out but, if Dad was that astute, they wouldn't fool him.

"To tell that woman how you feel."

"She'd have to let me get within ten feet of her for that to happen." James poked the pointy toe of his boot into the dust, sounding sullen even to himself. There was no point in pretending his father was wrong.

Dad chuckled. "You were within ten feet, right over there by the corral."

"Emotionally, she might as well have been at the north pole."

"You two used to be such good friends. What happened?"

A good question, and one that James had mulled over many times. He shook his head slowly. "I'm not sure. She started poking at me about dating two or three years ago. She's had no shortage of options to present, and I can't convince her to stop." Although today's retaliatory scuffle may have done the trick. "Honestly, her obsession makes it hard to talk to her anymore."

"So, why's she doing that? Pushing you away?"

"I wish I knew."

"Is she matchmaking anyone else?"

James shrugged. "Not this much. She had a few suggestions for Kade last summer before Cheri returned, and Garret sounded disappointed Lauren didn't care enough about him to give him more of a push. I seem to be special." Yeah, he sounded bitter. Sue him.

Dad laughed. "About what I thought."

"That doesn't even make sense."

"Doesn't it? Think on it a little deeper, Jamie. Pray, too."

Yeah. Sure. Like he hadn't been doing either of those things all along.

Dad turned on the golf cart. "Tori tells me Cabin Two is ready for guests. I was going to go have a look. Join me?"

"Okay." James walked beside the cart, thankful for the help the battery-powered vehicle offered his father in getting around the ranch. The bonus was it doubled as a luggage trolley for guests who brought everything but the kitchen sink on their vacations.

At Cabin Two, Dad took his crutches and slowly maneuvered up the few steps to the deck.

"Still thinking of building four more cabins next year?" James asked.

Dad nodded and pointed up the lakeshore. "On the other side of the canoe storage shed, I think."

"How about we make one or two of those wheelchair accessible?"

"Now there's an idea." Dad tapped a crutch against his leg and looked out over the small lake. "Might be folks like me looking for a taste of ranch life or accompanying able-bodied families."

"That's what I was thinking. Ground level entry, wide doorways, no-threshold showers. That kind of thing." All the adjustments the ranch house had required after his father's accident.

Dad turned from the railing. "I appreciate the thought, Jamie. You've got a good heart."

"Are you sure we can do that and build a house for me?"

"Went over it all with the accountant. The Flying Horseshoe is solid, son, thanks to you and your sisters stepping up when your mother and I needed you most."

James followed his dad into the cabin's living room. "This ranch means everything to all of us kids. We'd do anything to take care of it. To take care of you."

"We're blessed." Dad swiped at his eyes. "I can't tell you how sorry I am you had to give up your dreams of finishing college. Your sisters never even got started."

Time to lighten the mood. "Meg wasn't exactly aiming for a degree in anything fit for civilization."

"No. No, you're right. Thankful she found her way back to God, though. That's what is most important." He paused, looking around. "Looks good in here. Tori's got a good eye. You should get her to give you a hand with your house."

"And let the high praise go to her head? I don't think so." James laughed. "I do like this color of paint, though. I was thinking of going with the wooden wall option but both Denae and Tori are against it."

Dad turned, eyebrows up. "Denae?"

"Denae Archibald. Stewy's daughter. You remember Stewy and Michelle used to own Standing Rock? Denae is back in Saddle Springs."

"And she has an opinion because...?"

"She popped into Java Springs the day I had the preliminary meeting with Brent Callahan. I invited her to make some suggestions."

"Do you care for this Denae?"

James shrugged. "Not really. She's renting the other half of Lauren's duplex. They're friends."

"Then why involve her?"

"Why not? She's a woman. I needed a female perspective."

"There is no such thing as a female perspective." Dad shook his head. "Where did I go so wrong with you?"

What was that supposed to mean? James glared at his father. "Every guy thinks solid wood walls are a terrific option. Every woman I've talked to says the interior walls should definitely be sheet rocked and painted. If that's not a differing gender perspective, I don't know what one is."

"Just because something is usually true doesn't make it a law for all women. What if Lauren Yanovich is the one in a thousand women who prefers wood, but you didn't ask her?"

James drew himself to his full height and looked down at his father. "I don't know why you're back around to this."

"Oh, I think you do, Jamie. I think you do." Dad shuffled through to the kitchen, nodded as he glanced around, then returned to the glass doors to the deck. "Looks good, son. Thank you."

Chapter 10

"Oh, this place is adorable!" Denae peered up the ladder to the loft in James's cabin.

Lauren shifted on the leather loveseat. She generally avoided coming in here. It was compact, way too intimate. Not that she'd need to worry about James taking advantage of her presence when all he did was ignore her or treat her like one of the guys. She wouldn't be here now except that Tori had called everyone together to make final plans for the trail ride next week.

James stood in the archway to the dinette, blocking the view of the stables across the driveway behind him. She'd rather look at James, anyway, but not when he was focused on Denae.

"May I peek?" Denae pointed upward with a grin of glee right up there with a kid adopting a new puppy.

"Sure. Nothing much up there, mind you." James shrugged.

Denae didn't seem to care. She scurried up the ladder

and out of sight. "Oh, great space, James! Such an amazing view. Imagine lying in bed and gazing out at the mountains like this." Her shoes clipped the wooden floor overhead.

Who said things like that about a single guy's bedroom? Who even invited themselves into it? Lauren had helped clean the guest cabins a time or two in years gone by, so she had a fair idea of the layout of the loft in this one, but she'd never be this forward.

"Yeah, I like it." James didn't move.

Tori edged past him with a tray of drinks. "I'm after Mom and Dad to let me move in here when Jamie moves into his own house."

Garret looked up from poking at his phone where he sprawled in the one easy chair. "Is that a done deal then? What's the timeline?"

Was it Lauren's imagination, or did James's gaze skitter over hers?

"Looks like it. Dad signed a contract with Brent from Timber Framing Plus. They'll get started over the summer and fall when they're waiting on things at Kade and Cheri's. Hopefully they can get to lockup before snow flies and do the finishing work over the winter."

Denae scrambled down the ladder. "Their place will be amazing. Cheri showed me some of their choices. She has such an artistic eye, that girl."

Of course, Denae had her fingers in everyone's pies. Why was Lauren irritated at the thought? She was the one who'd kept in touch with Denae, the one who'd invited her to move back to Saddle Springs. Tried to turn James's attention to her.

"Did you see the mural Cheri painted this winter at the public library?" James asked Denae. "She's all self-taught, too."

Well, Lauren had succeeded, it looked like. Wasn't this what she wanted? To find someone for James? Denae might be annoyingly bubbly, but that might be a little jealousy poking through. She wasn't air-headed. She had a strong work ethic and had built up a solid editing business so that both traditional and independent publishers sought her out, willing to pay her fees.

Tori set out bowls of popcorn and passed out glasses of iced tea. "Dad also contracted Timber Framing Plus to build four more guest cabins. Those won't be ready until next season yet, though."

"I told him the guest cabins should come first, but he insisted." James lowered himself to the floor by the glass doors and snagged a popcorn bowl.

"He probably thinks there isn't a woman alive who'd want to live in a tourist cabin this size." Tori giggled. "He just wants to marry you off."

Denae sat cross-legged beside James and shook her head as he proffered his popcorn. How could anyone look that good in leggings and a tunic? Lauren tugged self-consciously at her sweatshirt. Maybe putting in more of an effort wouldn't be a bad idea, but she sure didn't have a pencil-thin supermodel body like Denae. That girl could wear anything and look like a million bucks.

Tori settled in beside Lauren, pen and notebook in

hand. "Okay, so we've got about seven hours on the trail Friday. I hope everyone has been riding enough to be in shape for that."

Uh. About that. Lauren really did need to buy her own horse and get out more. She was going to be saddle sore even after her bravado.

"Garret, are you trailering Trudy over that morning or the night before? I think the rest of us are riding Flying Horseshoe mounts."

"The night before, if you've got a vacant stall for her."

"Trudy?" Denae giggled.

Garret grinned at her. "Yep, Trudy. That's the name she came with."

"There's an empty box beside Luna's. That way she'll be fresh and ready in the morning."

"Sounds good." Garret nodded.

Tori consulted her notes. "We're taking two packhorses for all the gear. I have a tent big enough for us three girls, but you'll each need a sleeping pad and bag."

"Taking a tent, Carmichael?" Garret looked at James.

"Nah. There are lots of trees up there. I figured on hanging my hammock and sleeping under the stars. It's too early for mosquitoes."

"Not sure I'm up for that."

"So, bring a tent." James shrugged.

Guys. Seriously.

"I was thinking we'd try to get away around eight, so we have time for a couple of breaks," Tori went on. "And we'd be to the hot springs with enough time to set up camp before dark, cook and clean up supper, plus have a soak before bed."

"I'm going to need that soak." Lauren could already feel her aching muscles.

"Me, too." Denae sighed dramatically. "You said I could ride Pippi, right?"

Tori nodded. "We have the camp kitchen, but you all have been assigned your two meals to prep for." She pointed her pen at Garret. "That includes you."

He groaned. "I'm a terrible cook."

"There's no time like the present to learn."

"You'll all die."

Denae snickered. "What meals do you have? You can have my first lunch on our ride up the mountain. Bring something portable."

His face brightened. "Really? Thank you. You can have my Saturday breakfast instead. I burn fried eggs every single time, and that's on an electric stove, not over a campfire."

"Wait. We're cooking over a fire?" Denae's wide eyes scanned everyone in the room.

"Sure are. I know I told you that."

"I take back my offer. I'll do lunch."

"Too late." Garret drummed his fingers on the chair's arm, grinning smugly.

"Okay, Garret is supplying Friday lunch. I'm on Friday supper." Tori scribbled in her notebook. "Denae has Saturday breakfast. Lauren's got lunch, and James has supper." She rattled off the remaining two days. "We'll have a grill for over the fire, frying pans, and a cast iron

Dutch oven. Plus, a kettle for heating water and a campfire percolator, since none of us can survive without our morning coffee. The camp kitchen includes plates, bowls, utensils, all that sort of thing. Bring your own thermal mug and water bottle. Any questions?"

"I'm on Sunday lunch," Garret said. "How long will ice packs last to keep stuff cold?"

"Double zip lock anything that needs to keep chilled. We'll hang a mesh bag in the creek."

"But it's a hot spring."

"Only the one. The others are glacier-fed."

Lauren couldn't help watching James as the conversation danced around them. He leaned back, braced on both arms, with his jeans-clad legs crossed at the ankles in front of him. If he were aware of Denae's knee brushing his thigh, he showed no sign of it.

Denae said something — Lauren missed the question — and James turned toward her to reply.

Jealousy stabbed Lauren like a maddened criminal making sure his victim was truly dead. She hadn't thought it would hurt this much, getting James interested in someone. How was she going to manage four days watching them? By the end of it, they'd be holding hands and kissing in the bushes. She knew it.

JAMES SHIFTED ON THE FLOOR, just enough to allow airflow between his leg and Denae's. If she was coming on to him, it was subtle. Maybe this was just her way, being loud and excitable and not paying attention to personal space. Her voice seemed rather high-pitched, and she giggled far too much. There was no way on earth he could envision a life with her by his side.

Finally, Lauren turned toward Tori in conversation, and he could watch her without feeling weird. Something about oats for the horses in case there wasn't enough grazing near the hot springs. His sister could handle it. He didn't have to pay attention.

He envisioned Lauren in the dress she'd worn as Cheri's bridesmaid two months back. Did she know how stunning she looked in it? He longed to tell her how beautiful she was, how much he loved her short springy curls and gorgeous smile. He longed to tell her he loved her and let the chips fall where they may. If he could gather her in his arms and kiss her the way he dreamed of, she'd believe him. Would she push him away? Laugh in his face?

At some point, he needed to take that risk. Maybe sometime on the camping trip, even though it was still two months until their birthday. He probably didn't need to wait, right? What was the worst that could happen? Doc Torrington would take over as the Flying Horseshoe's veterinarian. Lauren had already stopped singing on their worship team, so nothing would change there.

What he'd lose was hope. He'd lose his fantasies of Lauren looking at him — really looking, for once in her life — with love shining from her eyes. He'd lose all his dreams. Men had survived that before, hadn't they? Somehow managed to put one boot in front of the other and carry on as though their hearts weren't smashed into powder. Maybe someday when he was forty or fifty he'd meet someone else and discover a shadow of the love he harbored for Lauren.

"Right, Jamie?"

He blinked at his sister. "Pardon me?"

Tori rolled her eyes. "You fixed the straps on the pack saddle last fall, didn't you?"

"Yes. Yes, I did."

"If you could focus for just half an hour, we'd be done here, and we could play a round or two of cards."

"No, I've got a super early morning tomorrow." Lauren covered her mouth in a yawn.

Was it fake? Was she trying to get away?

"Me, too," put in Denae. "A rush job just came in this morning, so I need to finish it plus the novel I'm already half done before Friday."

"A rush job?" Garret laughed. "What's so urgent about editing?"

"Goes to show what you know." Denae grinned at him. "For the authors, it's life or death. Seriously, the drama. I've got my regular clients organized enough to book me ahead and get their manuscripts in on time, but this newbie is willing to pay extra for a quick turnaround on a novella, and her sample is well-written and intriguing. I couldn't turn her down."

"Who knew?" Garret shook his head.

"Do you read?"

"I read music," he deadpanned.

That annoying giggle again. "That's not quite the

same thing. What kinds of stories do you like? Westerns? Thrillers? Fantasy? Action adventure? I can make some recommendations."

"Who's got time for that?"

James stuck his hand in the air and laughed when Lauren, Tori, and Denae did the same.

Garret scowled as he looked at James. "Always thought reading was a girl thing."

"Nope. A bit of escape is fun from time to time."

"Huh. You edit all those kinds of books?"

Denae shook her head. "No. I edit romance and some of its sub-genres, but I read other genres for fun."

"Romance?" Garret's eyebrows hiked up. "Like, smut?"

"Um, no. Like feelings. Emotions. The books I edit are from a Christian worldview so, while the couple is definitely physically attracted to each other, they're generally saving sex for marriage." Denae's finger made a circle around the room. "Like probably all of us are."

James swallowed a laugh at the red creeping up Garret's face. Poor guy didn't know where to look.

Tori cleared her throat. "Okay then. On that cheery note, shall we get back to business?"

"Please," mumbled Garret.

Across the small room, Lauren stared down at her fingers fidgeting in her lap.

James reached into his popcorn bowl, only then realizing it was empty. He definitely didn't need to be thinking about sex, whether it was fictional or real. Not when he was already struggling with how to treat Lauren and when and how to reveal his love for her.

What was the scripture about taking every thought captive to make it obedient to Christ? He needed to look that up and meditate on it. Maybe it was one of those 'God's will' verses he could add to the ever-lengthening list in the church's Facebook group. Had anyone made note of Philippians 4:8? He hadn't checked for a few days. That one definitely qualified. *Whatever is true, whatever is noble, whatever is right, whatever is pure, whatever is lovely, whatever is admirable — if anything is excellent or praiseworthy — think about such things.*

Dad's reminder to pray about the situation filtered into James's subconscious. To really ask for God's will and His direction rather than begging like a kid at the candy counter.

Every thought captive. *Please, Lord.*

Chapter 11

Lauren had never been so glad to see a waterfall in her life. It wasn't only because it was stunningly beautiful, though it was, but because her butt and thigh muscles screamed with mind-numbing pain after three hours in the saddle. It wasn't Luna's fault. The mare had picked her way up the trail, surefooted and steady.

It was Lauren's fault. She'd like to blame James for the fact that he stood as a barrier between her and riding, but that was stupid. She could ride at Canyon Crossing Stables. Or she could saddle up at the Flying Horseshoe and simply ignore James.

Ignoring James was difficult, though. He led the group, so she'd stared at his back all morning. She'd memorized the tilt of his black hat, the collar of his denim shirt above the maroon University of Montana sweatshirt, the jeans stretching down to the worn heels of his brown cowboy boots. He sat the saddle easily, like he'd been born to it, like he'd ridden every day of his life, which was probably true.

He slid off Jigsaw, the pinto's dark tail swishing against her splotchy flanks as her ears twitched toward the sound of running water. Beside Lauren, Tori dismounted from Coaldust, looking as fresh as she had hours ago. Obviously, Garret rode often as well. He gathered Coaldust's reins along with Trudy's and led them toward water. Denae groaned dramatically as she dismounted Pippi.

Lauren had yet to swing her leg over. She wasn't sure she could move those muscles, but she also couldn't stay on Luna through their break — to say nothing of another three or four hours. She edged Luna around so the horse's bulk shielded her from everyone's view, braced herself in the left stirrup, and tried to lift her right leg.

Oh, man. How had Denae managed? A glance showed Denae bent over with Tori patting her back. But James's eyes were on Lauren as he looped Jigsaw's reins over a bush. He took a step toward her.

No. She needed to get this done by herself. Lauren closed her eyes, braced herself, and forced her body to flex in all the required joints. She stumbled against Luna's side when she hit the ground, but strong hands caught her. "You okay?"

James. Of course, James. He let her go immediately, and she missed the fleeting warmth and strength. "Haven't ridden much over the winter."

"This is a brutal way to get back in the saddle."

She could hear the grin in his voice. "I'm holding on

for the hot springs. Gonna need that tonight." And a few painkillers.

"Yeah, me, too. Let me take Luna for a drink, and you find a place to sit down for a few minutes. Or walk and stretch."

"Okay."

He took the reins, and she forced herself to turn to the other girls rather than watch him walk away. "Gonna live, Denae?"

"It's debatable." Her friend looked back down into the valley with longing in her eyes. "Seriously thinking of making a run for it, but even that doesn't sound possible."

Tori giggled. "You'll be fine. We're over halfway, and there are hot pools at the other end. Think of immersing in soothing hot water up to your chin. You'll sleep like a baby tonight."

"On the hard ground."

"You have a sleeping pad to cushion you. Don't tell me you've never camped before."

"Dad and Michelle have a forty-foot RV."

"That's not camping."

"I never said it was. I might have slept in a tent a couple of times when I was a kid, in the vague and distant past."

Lauren turned as Garret came up beside them and tethered the two horses. "Anyone hungry?" he asked.

"I could eat a horse." Tori groaned then patted Coaldust. "No offense."

Garret chuckled and dug into the packhorse's saddlebag. "Sub sandwiches all around. Picked them up just before The Munching Moose closed yesterday."

Lauren shook her head. "Cheater."

"What?" He gave her a wide-eyed look. "No one will get poisoned this way. I put an ice pack in there." He handed a plastic-wrapped bun to Denae. "Hope everyone likes ham and cheese."

Denae held the package in front of her like it was a bomb with a ticking timer. "I don't really eat white bread."

"Uh... didn't I say sandwiches at our meeting last week?" He tipped his eyebrows up.

"Don't worry. The calories won't stick to your hips." Tori unwrapped her sandwich as James returned with the other horses. "You've burned off more than this already today."

Lauren peeled the plastic off her sub. No wonder Denae looked like a stick with a few minor bumps along it. Bread was a totally valid food group, right? Didn't matter what color. The bun had gotten a bit squished, but it still tasted like heaven.

Garret pulled a warehouse-sized bag of potato chips out of his backpack, tore open the top, and held it out to Denae. She blinked.

Tori's hands clamped on her hips. "Garret. Have you ever heard of nutrition?"

"Uh..." He looked at her, down at the bag, then up. "Yeah?"

"This isn't it."

James reached past his sister and came back with a

handful of chips. "Turn a bachelor loose with the instructions *bring lunch* and this is what you get."

Denae opened her sandwich and picked out a bit of meat.

Oh, good grief. Lauren inhaled the last of her sub, wishing Garret would offer another... or that Denae would share hers if she wasn't going to eat the thing properly. She snagged a handful of chips. "I don't remember anyone assigning a specific menu."

"It's like I thought you were all grownups or something." Tori glared at Garret.

"What? Grownups eat chips. I don't know what your problem is. James gets it, right, bud? What are we eating on your watch?"

"I, uh, brought steak and foil-wrapped potatoes. Might've tossed a whole cucumber in the saddlebag to slice up in lieu of salad."

"You're actually *cooking?*" Garret's voice echoed in disbelief.

"I kind of like to eat." James said it like an apology, as though he'd broken some kind of man-code. "And it's not like I have an imagination or anything. It's just going to be bacon and eggs and hash browns on my breakfast. I'm baking extra potatoes for that."

"Sounds great." Lauren took a swig from her water bottle, wishing it were a diet cola. "There's nothing better than steak cooked over a fire."

Tori and Denae both shook their heads at the chips as Garret offered them another time. Denae picked the scrawny scrap of limp lettuce out of the mayo and ate it while Tori balled up her plastic wrap and shoved it in the bag the subs had been in.

James angled a glance at the sun. "We should get going. Anyone need a bathroom break first? Girls that way, guys this way." He pointed as he spoke.

Denae gulped, and Lauren felt a flash of pity as she slung an arm over her friend's slim shoulder. "You're not in a motorhome anymore, Toto. Come on."

CAMPING with the gang hadn't been this much trouble when they were all eighteen or twenty. Telling everyone what meals they were responsible for had once been enough. No one cared what it was back then, but now, some of them had grown up and some of them hadn't.

James didn't even want to know what Garret had brought for his other meal, and a swarm of dread flooded his gut when he thought of Denae cooking for hungry campers. Hopefully she didn't think they all ate like grasshoppers. At least Tori and Lauren could be counted upon.

He sat staring into the fire as darkness and chill sifted over him. How had his sister talked him into this, anyway? It wasn't the same as before with Lauren, Kade, Cheri and some of their childhood friends, most of whom had gone off to college and never returned. And back then, things had been easy with Lauren. They'd been friends. What were they now? He wasn't sure.

Lauren sat on a downed log across from him, firelight

flickering on her pretty face and dancing off the tangled curls peeking out from her hoodie. She laughed at something Denae said.

James's heart ached. Back then, he'd been so sure that it was only a matter of time before Lauren would see him the way he saw her. She'd dated some in college, but he'd still held out hope. She'd returned to Saddle Springs and taken over her dad's half of the veterinary clinic. They'd still hung out, though she was definitely a lot busier. So was he, taking over more and more of the responsibility of running the Flying Horseshoe as the reality of his own father's limitations sank in.

Here they were, less than two months to thirty, and they'd drifted so far apart it was physically painful. For the first time in nearly fourteen years, he had to wonder if the pact would stand. What if she didn't love him? What if she'd rather stay single or hold out for someone who'd sweep her off her feet?

Garret shifted around in the shadows, assembling his flute on the makeshift camp table. A moment later, he ran through his scales then into the haunting melody of *Be Thou My Vision.*

Tori began to sing softly.

James closed his eyes and let the words wash over him. *Thou my best Thought, by day or by night; waking or sleeping, Thy presence my light.* He'd gotten hung up on thoughts of Lauren — again — when his focus needed to stay on Jesus.

Lauren's alto joined Tori's then a third voice lifted in a clear descant. Denae?

He looked across the fire and found Lauren's gaze on him but, before he could react, she turned away. What was she thinking?

Thou and Thou only, put first in my heart — High King of Heaven, my Treasure Thou art.

James knew all the words to every verse. He and Garret had led worship with this old hymn enough times. Practiced it dozens more. They liked to mix things up, newer worship songs with the classics. That way no one complained... except Lauren's mom, who inexplicably thought seventies-style choruses were the only way to go. But Dora Yanovich whined about everything, usually on high volume. How had Lauren turned out so well?

True to form, Garret shifted into a contemporary, *Trust in You.* James listened to the haunting music for a few bars before starting in on the lyrics. Why did it feel so much stranger singing these words at a campfire with Lauren across from him than in the sanctuary? He sang of letting go of his dreams and laying them in front of Jesus, crying out to Him, but trusting. Always trusting.

In reality, it was hard to hold onto wholehearted faith. No, he'd never faced the kinds of struggles some people had. No poverty, no broken home, no nights on the streets, no drugs. It should be easy for him to trust God when he'd never experienced true hardship.

Tori nudged another log into the flames. The fire crackled and hissed, popping sparks into the air. Wasn't it Job who said, *yet man is born to trouble as surely as sparks fly upward?* Yeah, no matter the circumstances, a guy's heart struggled.

Garret ran through the song again while the words echoed in James's mind. The last notes faded away.

"I like that one," Denae said softly. "Anyone else feel that way? Like you have all these questions you're asking God, and He doesn't seem to answer?"

Tori poked a long stick into the fire, shuffling the logs. "I think we all do, sometimes."

"That's why this song is popular." Garret laid the flute across his knees. "It describes a universal struggle, where we fight and push and try to win the battles on our own when what we really need to do is remember God's got it covered and trust Him."

"Then why do I feel so alone sometimes?" Denae picked up a small branch and began snapping it into pieces with her fingers. "I mean, I believe you. It makes sense, but that doesn't change my feelings."

Tori shifted on the log. "It's that whole divide-and-conquer thing. Satan wants us to feel alone, like no one else could possibly understand because they're all so much more spiritual than we are. We feel like we missed something simple and obvious, so we sit on it silently, hoping to figure it out before anyone else notices how depraved we are. While they are probably doing the same thing."

Bam. Welcome to the inner world of James Carmichael's thoughts. His sister had nailed it in one.

"If that's really true..." Denae's voice trailed off. "Then why don't we get over it? Really share our struggles with those close to us?"

"You first," quipped Garret.

James peeked a glance at Lauren. She leaned forward,

staring into the fire with her hands stuffed into her kangaroo pocket. What was she thinking? He'd rarely had to wonder in years gone by, because she announced her thoughts to everyone. Not lately, though. She'd pulled in.

He had, too. Oh, he'd never been as extroverted as Lauren, but his friendships had been... easier. He knew what had changed in him, that ever-increasing awareness that his time was running out with Lauren. What had changed in her?

His heart skipped a beat. Was it the same thing? Remembering his promise on her sweet sixteenth? But there was no return spark that he could discern so, if that's what it was, her pull-back must be from dread.

Why hadn't he just gone for it a year or two ago, before the pressure mounted?

Chapter 12

"What's it like, being so close to thirty?"

Lauren opened one eye to see Tori watching her through the steam of the tarp-lined hot pool. Nearby, Denae sat on a rock at the edge with only her legs in the water. She wore a white bikini that showed off her ribs, with her long hair wound around her head in a braid to keep it out of the water.

Why couldn't Tori ask pointed questions of someone else?

"When I was a kid, I thought thirty-year-olds were decrepit old people with one foot in the grave." Tori laughed. "And now I'm only five years out, and I'm not feeling quite so ancient. So, I'm curious if you have any regrets. Any advice."

Lauren had only one question for James's sister, but she couldn't ask it. Did Tori know about the pact? She'd have been eleven when it happened, so it was unlikely... unless James had told her. Which was also unlikely, considering he'd stepped back the very next day and never mentioned it again to the best of Lauren's knowledge.

Denae swished her legs, rippling the surface of the little pool. "Yes, do tell."

The men had taken the packhorses back into the forest to haul in a few dead trees to buck up for the fire. The whine of the chainsaw could be heard in the distance, so Lauren knew James wouldn't overhear if she confided. It was slightly tempting, but no way.

She looked over at Denae. "Like I'm so much older than you."

"A year and a half." Denae sighed. "I've always wanted to be married before I'm thirty."

"Is that why you moved back to Saddle Springs?" Tori wanted to know. "Because you didn't see any prospects in Missoula?"

"Is it dumb? I edit romance novels every day, and I just can't help but believe in the dream. If all those characters can overcome the obstacles in their path and find their happily-ever-afters, why can't I?"

Lauren fought the urge to roll her eyes. "Because they're not real people? There aren't that many perfect guys out there." Even James wasn't perfect. Quite.

"So that's what happens when you're almost thirty." Tori laughed. "You turn all cynical."

"Don't you want to get married, Lauren?" asked Denae. "Is being a veterinarian all you ever dreamed of?"

She'd dodge the first half of that, thanks. "You make it sound like a nightmare instead of a dream."

"That's not what I meant. For my dad, all he ever wanted was to be an attorney. He didn't want to be saddled with my mom and me when I was a baby. He did manage to find time to fall in love with Michelle later, and she was the one who wanted to buy the ranch." Denae grimaced. "Dad only lasted a few years before he needed to be back in the city, back in the thick of things. He still works way too much. I know Michelle misses the ranch a lot."

"Somehow it's always been more acceptable for a man to be consumed by his career than for a woman," Tori observed. "That's one of the things I like about my parents owning a ranch. They share a career and work together."

"My parents didn't work together on anything." Lauren thought back to all the fighting. "The more Mom nagged, the longer hours Dad worked. He often took me with him, which made Mom even more upset."

"And then he died," Tori said softly. "I'm sorry if I'm dredging up bad memories."

Lauren shook her head. "It's okay. I guess that's one reason I've never bought into the dream, though. Sure, if the right guy came along…" And his name was James Carmichael. She blinked. "But I wanted to follow in my dad's footsteps, not sit around waiting for a man to make my life complete." Especially not a guy who only sorry for her lot in life, like Conor.

"It's only Jesus who can fill those empty spots, anyway, like we talked about last night at the campfire." Tori slid further into the pool, the water covering her shoulders.

"I think we can have those dreams and still be a good Christian." Denae's voice had an edge to it. "Wanting a husband and family isn't anti-spiritual."

"I didn't say it was." Lauren closed her eyes. "It's just not every woman's dream, like not everyone wants to be a vet. We're all individuals."

"Anyway, there seem to be a lot of single guys around Saddle Springs." Denae slid into the pool and gasped. "This is hot."

"Only 103." Tori nudged the floating thermometer in Denae's direction.

Now or never. "We even brought two of them on this trail ride," Lauren put in, eyes still closed. "Garret and James are both eligible. Both men who are seeking after God."

"Also pleasant on the eyes." Denae giggled.

"I've seen worse," Lauren agreed.

"I don't get why you haven't made a play for one of them yourself."

"Oh, Garret's too young for me." Lauren kicked herself mentally. Hard. Now she'd left herself wide open.

"How much does that really matter when you're out of school? It's not like he's eighteen."

"My brother isn't too young for you. You two share a birthday, right?"

"Um... yes."

"I didn't know! How romantic is that? If you two got married, he'd never forget your birthday."

"We're not getting married, so it doesn't much matter." Lauren got to her feet, swaying in the waist-deep water. "I should probably get lunch started. I haven't heard the chainsaw in a while, and the guys are sure to come back starving."

"But I just made it all the way in." Denae's lips pulled into a pout.

"Up to your waist isn't the same as all the way in." Tori sent a small wave toward Denae. "If you want love, girl, you have to dive in headfirst, no holding back. Right, Lauren?"

"How would I know?" Lauren clambered out and reached for her towel. "I'm sure the romance editor knows more than I do about how many different ways it happens for people."

"Oh, that's so true! It's one of the things I love about editing. Some characters do dive in, but of course there are always obstacles under the water when they do, because love doesn't come easy—"

"In stories," Tori interrupted. "Because readers read for the journey, not the destination."

"I think it's true in real life, too. Nothing worthwhile ever comes easy. Anyway, as I was saying, other personalities wade in slowly — that's more my style — and love finds them anyway. Still others get rolled over by a tsunami when they least expect it." Denae sighed. "Whichever way it happens, it's so romantic."

Lauren wrapped the towel around her waist and headed for the tent to get dressed before James had to see her in a swimsuit in broad daylight. No wonder she avoided girl talk anymore. Did James really deserve Denae's shiny-eyed views on love? Maybe.

And maybe not.

JAMES HAD DONE everything in his power to stay clear of Lauren all weekend, even if it meant dragging Garret into the woods to gather more firewood than they could possibly use in a week of thirty below. He justified it by reminding Tori this was a good spot to bring experienced ranch guests on trail rides over the summer. Now a neat row of chest-high split logs blocked the passage between two trees, further separating the guys' camping spot from the women's tent. They'd created a nice stash for upcoming campfires. His future self would thank him.

Tori and Denae cleaned up from their second last meal of the trip — his sister had cooked cornbread over the fire to go with the chili she'd brought frozen from home — and they'd break camp after breakfast in the morning. It couldn't come soon enough. Watching Lauren studiously avoid him felt like a hoof to the gut.

Tori packed the plates into the kit bag while Denae tossed the wash water into nearby shrubbery. Garret played the flute beyond the campfire, but tonight no one began to sing. Lauren seemed unbelievably enthralled with the flames.

James shifted, a knot on the log suddenly seeming to bite into his rear. Lauren glanced up, and their gazes locked. Something besides firelight seemed to flicker there for a few heartbeats, then her expression blanked. What had he done to turn her so completely away? The night of Rosebud's birth, he'd really thought they'd reconnected, that the chill of the past year or two had dispelled.

There'd been definite heat that night. Either that, or he had the world's best imagination. Which was laughably untrue. Not after listening to Denae's incessant chatter all weekend, and she was at it again. He tuned in, fully expecting it to be full of nonsense as usual but, hey, a guy could live in hope that she had real thoughts occasionally escaping that bubblehead.

"Is it ever okay to go back on your word? I know we're not to break vows to God, but we say all kinds of things in passing to other people that we don't really mean." Denae looked around the small group as she took a seat. "Or is that only me?"

"Not sure what you're getting at." Tori clipped the dishcloth and tea towel to the paracord James had strung between two trees. "My parents drilled into us kids that our word is our bond. If we say we're going to do something, we'd better do it, come hell or high water."

James closed his eyes. This was not a conversation he wished to participate in.

"But what if it was said in a moment of weakness, or as a prank, but the other person believed it?"

No. No, no, no.

"I guess it would depend on how it was said. Like if it was clearly a joke." Tori looked around. "Come on, guys, help me out."

Lauren shrugged as she picked up a twig and tossed it in the flame. "I've got nothing here."

Did that mean she didn't believe in keeping promises?

James knew she did. He couldn't think of a single time she'd said she'd do something but didn't. She was dependable.

Garret disassembled his flute. "Keeping our word is important. I guess I'd need more context as to why you think there might be times it isn't."

"Well, honestly, it's because of this story I was editing."

James dared to let out a breath. If Denae was in a fictional realm, everything was fine.

"Oh?" Garret rubbed a section of his instrument with a cloth.

"Yeah, the hero whispered promises to the heroine when he thought she was asleep, but she was only pretending to be sleeping, and she heard him. So, is he bound by them?"

"Sounds like a dumb story." Garret laughed. "If you're going to make promises, look someone in the eye and shake their hand or something."

Denae giggled. "People in romance novels do *not* shake hands, silly. The promises are sealed with swoonworthy kisses. At least, if the heroine is awake. That part of the story kind of bothered me, because he pretended he hadn't said anything for like half the book, and she pretended she hadn't heard for just as long. It didn't seem realistic to me as a plot device for keeping them apart, but the author disagreed with me."

"Well, if they're not ready for the kiss of death — I mean kiss of promise — then they should at least high-five on it. Right, Carmichael?"

James closed his eyes as his head fizzed and his limbs grew weak. No. Stinking. Way. How could Garret go there?

"High five?" Denae giggled. "That's hilarious, Garret. That never happens in romance novels."

"Then they're not like real life, I guess."

"Yeah, right. Name me one time that would even make sense in real life. Remember, we're talking about two adults who really care about each other, not two ten-year-olds."

The sound of an overturning log yanked James's eyes open as Lauren surged out of the circle. James jolted to his feet.

Denae and Tori both cast confused frowns in his direction, but Garret grinned at him.

"Thanks, buddy," James ground out. "Thanks a lot."

Garret winked. "Opportunity, meet golden platter."

"I don't think so."

"What on earth is going on?" asked Denae.

"Back in high—"

"Shut up, Morrison. Just shut up." James followed Lauren down the trail. Why couldn't there be a full moon tonight? She'd vanished into the long shadows among the trees. "Lauren?"

Silence.

Oh, man. What was he going to say when he found her? He'd better think of something quickly, because none of the scenarios he'd played out in his imagination had been anything like this one. This was reality. This was here. Now.

"Lauren?"

If his ears hadn't been super-tuned to the night sounds, he wouldn't have caught the sniffle or the crack of a twig over to his right. He moved in her direction. "Lauren, I—"

"Go away, James." Her voice was flat. Completely devoid of emotion.

"No, I think maybe we should talk."

"What, so Garret can have some fun with it? Nothing I like more than to be laughed at."

"That's not what happened."

"Oh? What other explanation is there?"

"Kade said something the other day about... about it, and Garret clued in. He probably thought he was being helpful."

"Yay."

Her voice was not yay. "Lauren, I've been thinking about that night. We did make a promise to each other. And look at us, we're both still single. I never thought that would happen, did you?"

Silence.

"I admit I always hoped it would, but I nearly lost faith when you dated that guy in college. And then—"

"James?"

His heart skipped a beat. "Yes?"

"Shut up."

"Shut... what?" Since when did a guy start baring his soul to the woman he loved, and she told him to stuff it?

"Forget about it. We were kids. I'm sure we're well

past the statute of limitations for stupid things said in childhood."

"Childhood? We were sixteen, Lauren. Not exactly infants."

"Old enough to know better. You're right... which changes nothing. I let you off the hook, and you do the same for me. Find some nice girl to marry, why don't you?"

But he didn't have time to wonder at the tone of her voice. Not when they finally acknowledged memory of that night — compliments of Garret — and she basically told him, "thanks, but no thanks." He'd dreamed of telling her how he'd waited for her all these years, how he loved her, always had, and she'd step into his arms. He'd kiss the smile right off her face.

Her elbow stabbed his ribs as she strode past him, but he caught her arm. "Lauren, wait. Please."

"Are you kidding me?" She jerked her arm free and stared up at him, her face in the deep shadows. "I'm not a pity project, James Carmichael. I wasn't one fourteen years ago, and I'm not now. I happen to like my life the way it is. I keep crazy hours as a vet, and I find my work very fulfilling. I don't need you or anyone else coming along to rescue me."

"Res-rescue you?" Why couldn't his brain catch up? He rocked back on his heels as she brushed past him. "Lauren..."

But she was gone.

Chapter 13

Lauren slipped into the tent long after the camp had settled, sliding the zipper as quietly as she could.

"Lauren? You okay?" whispered Tori.

Did she have to answer? Why couldn't her friends be asleep? She stifled a groan.

"Garret told us what happened. He feels super bad about it."

He should. She'd like to deck him with a two-by-four. Garret... or maybe James. Or both. All men, everywhere.

"Did you and James kiss and make up?" whispered Denae eagerly. "Will you be married before your birthday to keep your pledge?"

Both of them were awake? Great. "I don't want to talk about it." Lauren stripped off her jeans and fumbled in her backpack for her sweats.

Tori's sleeping bag rustled. "My brother bungled things, right?"

Hadn't Lauren just said she didn't want to explain? She felt around for her fuzzy socks and tugged them on then slid into her down bag.

"He did, didn't he? Men can be so obtuse."

"This is like the black moment in a romance story, when all hope is lost." Denae's voice rose a little. "In the morning, everything will look better. He'll come to his senses, kiss you passionately, and you'll live happily ever after."

Lauren couldn't help the snort that erupted. "Real life isn't like your stupid books. Sometimes when everything goes wrong, it means that everything went wrong. The end. Besides, I don't want to get married. Not to James, not to anyone."

"You don't?" whispered Tori. "I keep catching you and James watching each other, and I was pretty sure that, one of these days, you'd both realize you were in lo—"

"We're not in love," hissed Lauren. "Get this stupidity out of your mind." Wait. Had she just called both her best friends stupid? She was the moron. Lauren pulled a sigh from the depths of her soul. "I'm sorry. I shouldn't be taking it out on you two. But can we just drop the subject? Please?"

There was silence for just long enough that Lauren hoped they agreed. But, no.

"I just have one question," whispered Denae. "Is it true? That James promised to marry you if you were both single at thirty? That you high-fived on it as teens? Because that's super awesome and, yes, swoon-worthy."

"It's *not* swoon-worthy. I don't know how many ways to explain this. There's nothing romantic about a high-five."

"I'm not so sure. Like Tori said, James is always watching you." Denae giggled. "Not in a creepy way. More... protective, I guess. Like he'd come unglued if you began dating someone else."

Unglued? Ha. Right. "I'm not dating anyone else. Didn't you hear me? I don't want to get married. Not to anyone." Why did she keep lying? Why did they push her to keep lying?

"That's an idea," came Tori's voice. "We'll set you up with someone else and see what happens. I bet Garret would play along. He really feels bad about blowing off the secret and putting you both on the spot."

"Garret? Hmm. No, it should be some new guy to town. Tall, dark, handsome, and mysterious. A bit brooding, like Heathcliff or Mr. Darcy."

If that didn't fit James Carmichael to a tee, Lauren would eat her boots. He hadn't always been this moody. There'd been a lot of laughter until the last year or two. She hadn't known what to make of the gradual change in him. At first, she'd chalked it up to shouldering more responsibility as his dad's situation became clear, that Bill Carmichael would never walk freely again. It was more than the specialists had expected that the man could get around as well as he did. But, as time had gone on, James's despondence had only grown. It couldn't all be about his father.

Could it be about her? What had he said, that he'd

always hoped she'd still be single, so he could make good his pledge? Where was the love in all that? She'd dreamed of it, but he only felt he needed to keep a promise. No wonder he seemed to be depressed and avoiding her. It was the burden of feeling forced to marry her that weighed so heavily on him.

At least now she knew and had released him from his promise. She should sleep well tonight with that load relinquished. Ha. Right.

If only Garret hadn't opened his mouth. There really was little James could have said right after that segue. But, if he actually loved her, why didn't he say it? Would she believe him? Probably not. *Thanks for nothing, Garret.*

"...maybe Sawyer Delgado?"

Lauren's thoughts riveted on Tori's whisper. What? No. "Stop it. Sawyer's an annoying kid. Besides, he's married to the rodeo circuit. I have zero interest in him. Less than zero."

"Yeah. I doubt he'd play along, plus we'd have to explain everything. I guess it has to be Garret. I think he'd do anything to make up for this."

"Would you two quit meddling?" Lauren allowed her voice to show the irritation welling up in her. "I mean it. I'm not interested in dating." Only James, who couldn't do anything right. Only James, now lost to her forever after his dumb words. After Garret's. After her own.

Everything in her longed to tiptoe over to the hammock way over by the hot pool and tell James she was wrong. She loved him, always had, she just hated being pushed. But the outcome her soul craved — the one with toe-curling kisses and murmured endearments and passionate caresses that would satisfy all her doubts — wouldn't be there. He'd be all, "sure, yes. Let's get married then. It'll be great."

Promise fulfilled.

She couldn't bear it. Her soul was already shriveled into a quivering mess, but to be married to a man she desperately loved but who didn't love her in return would squeeze the remaining life from her. She couldn't do it.

"I think that's a great idea. We'll talk about it more when we get back to town." Denae's yawn punctuated her words. "At least, if I survive the return ride."

And then there was all that physical pain to look forward to. Yay.

"I'm sorry, man." Garret held Trudy back at the end of the entourage where James rode, the two packhorses plodding behind him.

On Friday, life had seemed full of promise. Birdsong trilled in the trees around them, the sun shone on their backs, and the fragrance of fir trees' fresh, new growth filled the air with hope. James would be watching for a chance to tell Lauren how he felt.

Now? He'd rather knock Garret over the nearby cliff for all his interference. He'd been caught off guard and blundered everything. Why hadn't he just gathered Lauren in his arms out there in the woods and kissed her? Maybe that would have convinced her, but she hadn't given him a chance. She'd cut him off at every turn, pushed him forcibly away, and freed him from his promise.

He didn't want to be freed, but he also didn't want to marry her because of it. He wanted to marry her because he loved her. Why hadn't he said those words? He'd kicked himself half the night for not laying his emotions on the line. For not making her listen. For not kissing her.

He'd had so much practice holding back it had become his default, and he'd fumbled the opening. The really ignorant, dumb opening offered by his ignorant, dumb friend who rode beside him now looking like someone had killed his puppy.

James heaved a sigh. "What's done is done."

"I should never have opened my big mouth."

"Yup."

"I'm really, really sorry."

James closed his eyes for a brief moment as Jigsaw picked her way down the trail. Lauren, Tori, and Denae had disappeared around the next bend a few minutes ago. He did not want to have a heart-to-heart with Garret. He didn't want to have one with anyone, not even God. "You mentioned that." If Garret was looking for reassurance like, "it's okay," it'd be a long time coming.

"James..."

"Shut up, Morrison." He said it casually, no recrimination. But the guy needed to catch a clue.

"Okay. So long as you know—"

"I know."

Half an hour later they dismounted at the waterfall.

The three horses were tied to some bushes, and the women were seated on rocks facing the thundering water. If that wasn't a clear signal, James had never met one. He led the horses downstream to drink in a quiet pool.

When he returned to the clearing, Denae jumped up, opening a bag as she approached. "Lunch?"

He wasn't really hungry. He might never be hungry again, but he supposed he could eat something. He looked in Denae's bag then at her. "Pepperoni sticks?"

She nodded with a bright smile. "Low-fat. And cheese sticks, too. Plus, there are lots of broccoli florets and some energy bars."

"Low-fat pepperoni." Who knew there was such a thing. "Broccoli."

Denae peered up at him. "Yes, one of my favorite lunches. Only the broccoli looks a little wimpy after a few days. Sorry about that."

Maybe James had only thought he wasn't hungry. Now that he'd seen the meager offerings, he was starving. If he tried really hard, could he get the previous mindset back? He reached into the bag, pulled out four meat sticks and two of cheese. When Denae's eyebrows rose, he plucked out a small handful of broccoli. She was right. It had seen better days. He forced a smile. "Thanks."

"You're welcome." She beamed at him then scurried back to Lauren and Tori.

Garret stared at the pepperoni in his hand. "Makes a guy wish he'd had more of Lauren's pancakes at breakfast." Then his face brightened. "I've got a bag of cheese puffs in my saddlebags. Plus, a package of gingersnap cookies."

Denae glanced over her shoulder at them, and James made a show of popping the entire handful of broccoli in his mouth. He didn't generally mind it... freshly cut and loaded with ranch dressing. Or roasted in a ton of olive oil. He got it swallowed and gave Denae a thumbs-up. She smiled and turned back to the creek.

"You're a better man than I am," muttered Garret as he flung his few florets into the dense brush with the skill of a pro ball player. He rummaged in the leather bag strapped behind his saddle.

James stripped the wrap off a pepperoni stick and chomped the thing down in three bites. He'd had worse. He couldn't remember when, but it had to be true. Still, he wouldn't turn down cheese puffs or cookies. Or his mother's cooking tonight at supper.

FROM THE EVIDENCE her furtive glances revealed, their... *discussion*... last night hadn't dampened James's appetite any. Lauren didn't miss the bright orange bag passed back and forth between the two guys, but she wasn't about to point it out to Denae. Then she'd have to explain why she was looking in the first place.

Not going to happen.

James had eaten his allotment of six pancakes and four sausages for breakfast, dousing the works in a thick layer of butter and maple syrup. She'd made the pancakes a little too large and thus managed to short herself, but two was plenty. It wasn't like she was hungry, or ever would be again. Huh, in a year or two, she might even be as skinny as Denae. Not that she wanted to be, but getting rid of five or ten pounds would be okay.

She hated to admit it — and never would, out loud — but her friends had a point. The only way to banish James's ghost from her mind and emotions was to prove she didn't need him. Mom was always after her to give her short, curly hair a bit more shape, and she could dig out her makeup and wear some occasionally. Buy a few new outfits that weren't sweats. Go out with friends. Be vivacious. She'd once been the life of the party. She could do that again, right?

Life after James was going to look like everything she'd said was true. Like her life was full and complete and fulfilling. Because, by golly, it would be. She was only going to be thirty, not ninety. She had a lot of years left to go, and she was not going to spend them mourning the might-have-beens.

Any crying that needed to occur she'd do this week in the privacy of her own home. Then, look out world. The new Lauren would emerge like a phoenix from the ashes.

Now who sounded like she'd read too many novels? But no more romances for her.

Chapter 14

The first guests of the summer season would arrive at the Flying Horseshoe tomorrow. Their chef, Ollie, had his camping trailer parked behind the restaurant, the kitchen was stocked for the grand reopening, and the staff hired. Two teens — one of them Pastor Roland's son Matt — would be starting Saturday in the stables.

James could only be thankful he'd had to jump right into final preparations as soon as they'd returned from the trail ride a few days ago. The added benefit? The workload kept Tori off his back, since she was occupied with airing out the cottages and adding welcoming touches.

The florist van from Florabelle pulled up at Cabin Two just as he turned all the horses out into the nearest pasture, Rosebud dancing at Snowball's heels. James tipped his hat at the driver, headed back into the stable, and grabbed a rake off the hook on his way by. Come

Saturday, mucking out the stables would become the duty of the hired hands. Today it was still his.

Memories of Lauren assaulted him everywhere he turned. Snowball's box, where they'd labored together to deliver Rosebud. Luna's stall only reminded him of how strong and confident Lauren looked sitting on the black mare's back. He started on Luna's, raking the soiled straw into the alley, then splitting a fresh bale and kicking the flaps loose to form a clean bed.

God, what am I going to do?

How many times had he asked this in the past few days? But it wasn't even the right question. He knew that. The right question was, *God, what are* You *going to do? How can You be glorified in this?* But didn't that mean he needed to get over his anger and frustration with Garret for forcing his hand, with Tori and Denae for having witnessed it, with himself for bungling everything so badly? And yes, with Lauren, for not reading what he was trying to say. For not loving him in return.

That was the bottom line, yet he couldn't point at anything tangible to prove she'd led him on. She hadn't. She'd been pushing him away for years, pushing him toward other women. He hadn't known what to make of that at the time, but now it seemed apparent that she'd really meant it all but had been too polite to say, "James, I know we made this deal when we were kids, but I don't want to go through with it because I don't actually like you, let alone love you."

Yes, that would have crushed him, and he might not

have easily given up hope even then. But he'd have heard her words. Instead, all he'd received had been mixed signals. Verbally, she'd pushed him away, but then she'd looked at him with those dark, deep eyes, and he'd known she felt something for him, too, but wasn't ready to acknowledge it. He oiled the roller on Domi's stall door and slid it back and forth a few times to make sure it ran smoothly and quietly.

Maybe a shot of lubricant on his spiritual life wouldn't go amiss. Prayer. Reading scripture. Truly getting humble before God. James couldn't help wondering if the list of verses about God's will on Facebook included any that would speak to him now. Was there a scripture that gave a practical how-to-survive guide for a man who'd been dumped before he'd even had a girlfriend?

He'd pass on the verses about perseverance, thanks. He was done with patiently waiting. That ship had sailed, leaving him stranded in a storm.

"James?"

He pivoted, cracking his elbow on the metal edge of the door. "Ouch! Don't sneak up on people."

"Sorry." Tori stood in the aisle, misery clouding her face. "Can we talk?"

"I don't have anything to talk about."

"You can't keep everything inside you. That way leads to ulcers."

He shrugged.

"Garret feels horrible about what happened."

"He told me." About a thousand times.

"I can't believe I never knew that about you and Lauren. Who all was there?"

James turned and grabbed the rake then strode past his sister to the next stall. Started working.

"You're my big brother and I care about you, but you're about as easy to talk to as a brick wall."

Then she should give up.

"Harder, really, since a brick wall will never reply, but I keep holding out hope that you're actually human and might give in and say a few words."

James dug the rake tight into the corner and dragged it toward himself.

"Okay, fine. I'll talk to you, and you can think about it. I think you love Lauren, and I think she loves you."

The snort burst out before he could hold it back.

"Ah. A reaction. He lives."

"Go away, Tori."

"No, I don't think so. I've tried to give you some space, but we've been back three days and you're still sulking. I'm done with you pouting like Aiden when he doesn't get his way."

"Excuse me?" James pinned his sister with a glare. Only, she was right. He might not be able to match his young nephew's lower lip extension — the kid was a champ — but the point was still valid.

"You heard me. Man up, James."

"Look, you don't know anything, okay? Garret wasn't there. He got something like three sentences out of Kade one day. That's hardly a reliable source."

Tori dragged a bale to the middle of the doorway to

Domi's stall and plunked down on it. "Fair enough. You were there. You tell me."

She was right, though it killed him to admit it. He wasn't dealing with it well, bottled up like he'd done. He was so choked at numbskull Garret that it was all he could do not to toss him in with an angry bull. Who else was he going to confide in? Denae? Not likely.

Tori gave him an encouraging smile. Did she have any idea how hard this was for him?

James leaned the rake against the wall, took off his cowboy hat, and ran his hand through his hair before returning the hat. "I think I've loved Lauren since we were fourteen."

Surprise flickered in his sister's eyes for a brief instant. "That's a long time."

"Yeah. Her dad's death broke her, and her mom... well."

"Let's just say we're thankful Dora Yanovich isn't our mother."

He let out a humorless chuckle. "That about sums it up." Man, this was hard. "We started hanging out. Fishing. Boating. Innocent kid stuff."

Tori nodded.

"She was pretty excited when Dillon asked her out. I hadn't thought we were to that point yet. I mean, I didn't even have my driver's license, and I wasn't going to ask a girl out if we had to ride bikes or horses to get to the theater, right? Or worse yet, ask Mom or Dad to drive us."

"Plus, they said we couldn't date until we were sixteen."

"They decided that after Meg."

"Of course. And the only one it affected then was me, since Meg never met a rule she couldn't break." Tori's nose scrunched. "Anyway, carry on."

"Lauren wouldn't sleep with him."

"Of course not." Then Tori's eyes widened. "Oh. You're saying she... he..."

"He called her a baby and broke up with her the day before her sixteenth birthday."

"Which just so happens to also have been *your* sixteenth birthday."

"Yeah. So, we were having a party down by the lake. Kade, Cheri, a few other kids who don't live around here anymore. The moon was nearly full, and we were all goofing around out on the raft, but Lauren was super quiet. Bryce bugged her about why Dillon hadn't come to the party, and she finally spilled. She started crying about how she'd probably be an old maid because no one would ever want her just because he loved her."

"Oh, no."

In his mind, he was there. The shallow lake warm in mid-summer, the cool night air. The grumbles of a few ducks in the rushes along the water's edge, the fragrance of Lauren's vanilla-scented hair, the path of moonlight rippling on the dark lake. The murmurs of a few teenagers discussing the deeper points of life with all their adolescent wisdom.

"We talked about what *old* was, and we all agreed

thirty was the magic number. You got to three full decades without being married, and you were officially over the hill and barreling down the other side with no hope of love ever catching up."

His sister cracked a smile.

"I elbowed Lauren's arm and told her not to worry about it. If we were both unattached at that advanced age, we could always marry each other. She looked at me and said, 'really?' and I said, 'of course.' Then I raised my hand and she slapped it."

"And then?"

James shrugged. "Bryce pushed Cheri off the raft, and we all jumped in the water. I think we partied clear 'til midnight."

"That's not what I meant, Jamie. What happened next between you and Lauren?"

"Nothing really changed, except Dillon had moved on to the next girl. We all hung out, went riding, swimming, the stuff country kids do all summer. School went back in for junior year; life continued on."

"And no one mentioned the pact."

He shook his head. "I don't think anyone remembered for long. Except me... and, it turns out, Lauren. Kade had forgotten until that day he and Garret and I were in Java Springs a month or two ago. I don't know about Cheri or Bryce or the others."

"So, you've bided your time all these years."

"It sounds so dumb."

"It's kind of romantic, really."

He snorted. "It might be if Lauren hadn't told me to get lost."

"So. It's obvious to me that she loves you back."

James stared at his sister. "Did she say that?"

"No. Sorry. But I still think it's true."

"You've been hanging around Denae too much."

Tori offered a lopsided smile. "Could be, but here's the thing. She hasn't dated all this time, either."

"She had a boyfriend in college."

"Trust you to know that. But that was, what, five years ago? Ten? She was probably trying to move on, so you wouldn't think you needed to honor a childhood promise."

Lauren's voice rang in his mind. *I'm not a pity project, James Carmichael. I wasn't one fourteen years ago, and I'm not now.* He replayed that a few times, trying to remember the nuances, the expression on her face, the emphasis on which words. "Let's pretend for a minute that you're right."

Tori pumped her fist but remained quiet.

Thank the Lord for small miracles. "I was caught way off guard. Even though I hope I earned a point or two for following her Sunday night, I said all the wrong things."

"What did you say?"

James pulled the hat off his head and scratched his scalp. What *had* he said? "My plan, such as it was, was to start at the beginning by affirming the pact we'd made. That we might've been kids, but I meant it all the same."

"You're serious." Tori stared at him. "*That* was your big strategy?"

He winced. "I told you. I wasn't expecting the conversation to go there."

She shook her head, like he was the dumbest creature to walk on two legs. Maybe he was. "Okay, so what should I have said? Not that it matters anymore."

"Less talking. More kissing."

"What? *That* would have been your big strategy?" He mimicked her cadence from a moment before.

"For one thing, she'd have been so busy kissing you back, she wouldn't have been able to say mean things to you, which I'm sure she did. And for seconders, a kiss is worth a thousand words. She would have known how you felt, that you'd been waiting for her because you wanted her, not because you felt sorry for her."

Lauren had accused him of making her a pity project. Tori was right. James groaned and scrubbed his hand through his hair. "I can't believe..."

"Yeah. Me, neither. Here I thought Megan was the only Carmichael who had straw for brains. Now I know I'm the only one who doesn't."

That would call for a quippy comeback if it weren't so true.

"Look, the way I see it, you've got two choices." Tori tapped her jaw. "Or, I guess, three."

"Yes, oh wise one?"

She smirked. "You could always give up and let her go. Walk away. Forget it all."

James became aware of his head shaking. He'd spent fourteen years — and more — loving Lauren. It wasn't a faucet he could simply turn off.

"Or you could fight for her."

That sounded violent. Did he have it in him to push himself on her? "You said three choices. So far, I hear two."

"Well, there are two ways you can fight for her. You can start dating someone else — like Denae, maybe, or Carmen — and try to make Lauren jealous. Or you can sweep her off her feet with flowers and jewelry and dinners out."

He raised his eyebrows. "That's your big plan? Jealousy or extravaganza?"

"Yep." She nodded decisively as she rose from the bale and dusted her hands together. "What's it gonna be, big brother?"

Chapter 15

"Why weren't you in church? Are you sick?"

Lauren clutched her cat and stared at Mom standing on her doorstep, dolled up in her Sunday best. She should have known the inquisition was coming. "I've had a pounding headache for a few days." Which definitely was the truth.

"You look terrible." Her mother elbowed past her. "It's a good thing I came by to take care of you."

"I was about to go back to bed."

"You poor dear. What have you eaten today? Let me fix you something."

"I'm not hungry."

"But you need to keep up your strength." Mom's gaze slid the length of Lauren's body. "Chicken soup is low-calorie. Do you have some in the house?"

Wow, that had been subtle. Not. "There's probably a can in the pantry, but you don't have to do this. It's nothing rest in a darkened room won't cure." Felix reached up and patted her cheek with one black paw. He was better company than Mom by a long shot.

"A migraine?" Mom peered into the cupboard then shuffled cans and packages around.

No, but if this kept up, one was sure to explode soon. "Borderline."

"I'm sorry, sweetheart. Your dad suffered from so many of those."

The common denominator was Dora Yanovich. Coincidence?

"I don't see any chicken soup in here. I'm going to run over to Manahan's and pick some up. Anything else you need?"

Lauren rubbed her temples. She hadn't gone shopping since the trail ride except to pick up cream for the clinic.

Mom opened the fridge and tsked. "That package of baby greens is turning brown. And what's in all those Styrofoam containers?"

"Take-out." Which wasn't so different from normal.

"Didn't I teach you anything about cooking?"

The band around Lauren's skull tightened.

"Apparently I failed." Mom's lips pursed. "You're never going to catch a man if you don't know how to take care of yourself or your kitchen."

"I'm not trying to catch a man."

"Well, you should be. Growing old with no one by your side isn't a pleasant experience, I can assure you."

"Maybe you should remarry." The words popped out of Lauren's mouth without a detour through her brain. No man in his right mind... but wouldn't a romance of her own distract Mom from badgering Lauren? It might not be a bad idea.

"Don't be ridiculous. I loved your father."

"He's been gone half my life. I don't think it's a matter of how much you loved Dad. There's no reason to not even think about it. Wouldn't he want you to be happy and cared for?"

Her mother closed the fridge and leaned against the door as she surveyed Lauren with a piercing stare. "You're a fine one to talk, closing your mind to marriage without serious consideration."

"I have my career."

"And so do I. Speaking of which, your hair is getting shaggy. What day can you come by for a trim? Let's put some highlights in this time. I'll get Sabrina to do your nails while the color is setting."

Lauren looked at her hands. She kept the nails clipped short — a hazard of work — but maybe a bit of color wouldn't go amiss. "Sure. Whatever. Last appointment of the day on Thursday or Friday?"

Mom beamed. "I'll look at the schedule and text you a time. You won't regret it."

Yeah, she would.

"Then you'll be all prettied up to find yourself a date."

And the wheel had come full circle. "Tell you what.

You first. You start going out with some nice man, and I'll think about it."

"Done and done."

What? The headache squeezed. Felix growled. Apparently, her arms had squeezed, too. That was supposed to be a no-deal. *Like the one with James?* Lauren bit back a groan. Thinking before speaking was something she definitely needed to learn.

Mom patted her perfect hair. "I'll be back in a few minutes with soup. Have you taken painkillers? And maybe you should have a shower while I'm gone. It's amazing what a difference a little self-care makes." She breezed out the door.

Lauren stared after her, listening to the engine start and the car pull away from the curb. So much for wallowing in her own misery on her day off. Was it too much to ask? She hadn't been able to bear the thought of sitting in a wooden pew at Springs of Living Water next to Denae or Tori or even a stranger, should one happen to wander in. Listening to James and Garret lead worship, let alone participating. Ignoring his brooding gaze and pretending it had no effect on her.

But it did. And now, knowing James, he'd redouble his efforts to be a nice guy and prove he was a man of his word, even when it was uncomfortable. He might have spoken impulsively that long-ago star-studded night, but he'd stand by it.

Whereas Lauren had no intention of falling in line with a one-sided marriage. Maybe her mother's challenge was a godsend. Lauren would show James and all their friends that the night on the mountaintop hadn't affected her. She'd get busy dating, entertaining, laughing, and proving she was deliriously happy the way she was. She only needed to keep up the farce for six weeks, until their — *her* — thirtieth birthday. Then he'd feel off the hook and she could go back to... wallowing.

Unless the dating game turned out to be fun.

On the other hand, Mom hadn't dated since Dad, so what were the odds of her finding someone now?

Felix's paw tapped her cheek, and she buried her nose in his soft fur. This was the guy who knew all her secrets and loved her anyway.

"THE WEBSITE DIDN'T SAY anything about real cowboys." There was an appreciative whistle. "*Hot* cowboys."

The sultry voice came from behind James, but so close he couldn't pretend he hadn't heard, or that the woman was speaking to someone else. He lowered Domi's hoof and glanced over his shoulder. Whoops. Right at eye level with a pair of super-short jean shorts on shapely legs so tanned the color must've come from a bottle. Raising his gaze helped only marginally. The blond beauty had tied her gingham shirt at the waist. She must've picked up her fashion sense from the cover of a hot-rod magazine.

"Don't tell me you're taken." She draped herself across the stall door.

Domi whinnied and stepped sideways, rolling the whites of her eyes at the stranger. It might've been the powerful perfume wafting off the woman that had spooked the mare, but James was thankful Domi had given him a few extra inches to stand without bumping into her. He stroked the mare's shoulder. "James Carmichael." Did he have to shake her hand to be polite? Probably. He extended it. "And you are...?"

"Bailey Gabriel. I'm visiting from Chicago with a couple of girlfriends." Her gaze drifted the length of him and back up. "But I could be talked into more." She fluttered her eyelashes as she clasped his fingers between both hands and leaned closer. "What do you say?"

"I say no thanks." James tugged his hand free and tried to keep a generic smile in place.

She pouted. "Drat, you *are* taken. Though, of course, she'd never need to know...?" Her voice curled suggestively at the end.

"That's not how I operate." Why did he feel the urge to apologize for turning this brazen offer down? Politeness could be taken too far.

"We'll be here for two weeks in Cabin Nine, so you know where to find me if you change your mind."

Cabin Nine? Right next door. James's blood chilled. He'd never felt he needed to sneak into his own place before, but no way did he want Bailey to figure out where he lived... alone. Plus, he'd better start keeping his door locked, just in case.

"Are you and your friends scheduled for lessons or a trail ride today?"

"Only if you're there." She winked.

"I won't be." He turned back to Domi and nudged

the horse over so he could pick up her other hoof. "I hope you enjoy your vacation."

"That's the plan." Bailey giggled.

Did he dare send Matt out with this group? No. James didn't want to find out the hard way that Bailey or her friends weren't picky about a cowboy's age. Looked like Tori had just scored some hand-holding over the next couple of weeks. Lucky her.

"Girl! You look amazing. Let me see." Denae walked all the way around Lauren. "Your mom's a miracle worker."

Lauren shifted from one foot to the other. "Um… thanks. I think."

"No, really. Your hair has more bounce. Those curls! I'm jealous."

"There's so much more you can do with long, straight hair. If I let mine grow out, it mostly goes sideways."

Denae fingered her long strands. "At least yours has body. Mine just droops. But, seriously. I like the look. I didn't realize how long your hair had gotten until this cut." She grabbed Lauren's hand. "And look! Your nails are gorgeous. What's the event?"

"Nothing. My mom took over." As though that were something new.

"And here I thought it was so you could show James what he's missing."

Lauren shook her head. "That's not going to work."

"Because you've tried it? Don't give up. Not yet. Put

your heart on the line and make an all-out effort to snag that cowboy. What do you say?"

"I say you've read too many romances."

Denae smacked her arm gently. "Romance is real, silly. You don't have to read fiction to believe in happily-ever-after. Look at Cheri and Kade or Megan and Eli for examples. Look around at church on Sunday and see couples who've been together for ten, twenty, or even fifty years."

Both Cheri and Meg had gone through significant trauma on their way to true love with no guarantees they'd emerge married to their soulmates. Both had made every mistake in the book and found Jesus in the depths of their darkness. Then the light had shone, with Kade and Eli waiting to make the transitions complete.

Lauren hadn't made those huge mistakes. If that's what it took to find her heart's match, she'd live without him, thank you. She had plenty of beauty in her life even though James was a stubborn, misguided fool. She lifted her chin.

"Yay! We'll make it an event."

"Huh?" Lauren blinked at Denae.

"I could see your thought process as you decided to go for it with James. Now all we need is an actual plan. Let me see your closet."

"Um..." Her friend was delusional. No way was Lauren strolling up to James and telling him she'd loved him since they were kids and, yes, she'd accept his proposal if the offer still stood. But she could be the lifeblood of the party again and show the man what he was missing by taking her for granted.

The rattle of wire hangers from her bedroom caught Lauren's attention. She scooped Felix into her arms and followed Denae. "I don't have anything nice."

"Wow. You're not kidding. How many T-shirts and pairs of sweats does one girl need? And then there's this turquoise number." Denae pulled out Lauren's bridesmaid dress from Cheri and Kade's wedding and twirled it around. "This is uh-maze-ing, but it's a bit much for a night on the town. You don't have anything in between?"

"Jeans?" Lauren put a hopeful lilt in her voice as she dropped to the side of the bed.

Denae scowled at her with eyebrows raised. "I've seen your jeans. They put Michelle's mom-jeans to shame."

Heat crept up Lauren's cheeks as she clutched Felix to her chest. "I'm not skinny like you. Nothing looks good on me."

"Stand up. Put the cat down. Let me have a look at you."

Face burning, Lauren did as she was told, slowly pivoting at Denae's instruction.

"You've got curves. What're you hiding that bod behind baggy junk for?" Denae swept a pile of folded sweats into her arms. "Where's your garbage can?"

"No!" Lauren grabbed the stack and tried to tug them out of her friend's hands to no avail. "You can't trash my wardrobe."

"That's not a wardrobe, girlfriend. That's a smoke-

and-mirrors act to make you think you've got clothing. We're going shopping."

"No..."

"I'll loan you a few hundred dollars if you need it, though it will take at least a grand to get you properly outfitted. More like two. What day can we drive into Missoula? We could stay at Dad and Michelle's and take a whole weekend. I know some great little boutiques."

"I can't."

"I bet you can." Denae dumped the pile in the corner and tossed two pairs of jeans on top.

There wasn't much left besides the turquoise dress. Lauren eyed it. Once she'd gotten over the idea of the cross-pleated bodice and wide shirred waist and actually tried it on, she'd felt like a princess. The soft chiffon had swirled around her knees. She looked better than she'd expected in photos of the bridal party, even though the bright flowers she clutched in front of her didn't camouflage the fact that she was wider than the other bridesmaid or the bride.

Denae held up a gray T-shirt and scowled at it. "You know they make tees shaped for women, right? V-neck, trimmed in at the waist."

Lauren closed her eyes and let out a long breath. Was she going to let Denae do this to her? Throw away almost all of her clothes and bully her into spending a bunch of money on a new wardrobe? It wasn't as though her bank account was empty. The duplex was paid for, thanks to her inheritance from her father, so her biggest expenses were the Jeep and takeout. She tried to remember when she'd last gone on a clothes-shopping binge. College?

Maybe Denae was right. Maybe it was time.

And it had nothing to do with impressing James Carmichael.

Nothing much.

Chapter 16

"I don't know why I need to make all these decisions this far in advance," James grumbled as he anchored the corner of the blueprint with the napkin dispenser. "And I don't know why I need three bathrooms."

"Only three?" Kade propped his elbows on the table in Java Springs. "Don't let Cheri hear you say that, or any woman. I think our new house will have four. Or is it five, with the basement one? I've lost track."

"You're a big help."

"Besides, you know the answer. Yeah, one guy doesn't need that much space, but you'll have a family one day. We're still in the apartment above the garage while we're waiting for our house to be finished, and I can tell you I look forward to not having a kid pound on the bathroom door as soon as I get in there. Because when a kid's gotta go, he or she has seriously gotta go."

James skewered his buddy with a look. "Quit trying to make it sound like having kids is a downside."

"Yeah, well. I get it."

Did he? Kade hadn't hung around waiting for Cheri to come back into his life. He'd married Daniela, become the father of Jericho, and been widowed before Cheri returned to Saddle Springs. Lauren, on the other hand, had come home right after college and remained tantalizingly out of reach. Totally different scenario.

Kade peered at the paper. "Okay, so what decisions do you need to make right now? Something about bathrooms, I take it."

"Can they all be the same? I mean in finishes. Just one kind of cupboard and counter and tile and floor? Please?"

"You might want to put some upgrades in the master bath. Cheri's looking forward to a jetted tub." Kade tapped the blueprint. "Good, you've got a nice big shower in there. You'll appreciate that."

James didn't even want to know why. "Upgrades in the master bath. Got it. But… like what?"

The bells over the door jingled. Two females giggled. James froze, not daring to look up. Maybe they wouldn't recognize him here. He could hope.

"Oh, look, it's Mr. Hunky Cowboy!"

Bailey's voice. Great.

"Two of them," her friend countered.

James had already figured out that all three women were eager for exploits to regale their Chicago friends with after their vacation. He'd managed to avoid any one-on-one time since being caught in Domi's stall that first day. Now he and Matt made sure to work near each other, leaving Tori with the three blondes. It wasn't as efficient, but it was necessary.

The assault of Bailey's perfume warned him a second before she leaned over his shoulder, her hand with its red-painted nails splayed on the blueprint. "Oh, what have we here? Building a house, cowboy?"

"Or maybe your friend is?" Skylar all but crooned.

Kade shot James a tight, questioning look. "Excuse me. I don't believe we've met."

"I'm Bailey and this is my friend Skylar. We're staying at the Flying Horseshoe, but I see now we should have been spending more time in this quaint little town." Bailey pressed closer.

James took a deep breath. "This is my buddy Kade, and he's married."

Skylar offered a pout but didn't pull away.

"*Happily* married and father of two," Kade said. "And I'd really appreciate it if you'd take a step or two back."

The bells jingled again. With any luck it would be... James didn't know whose arrival would offer the salvation he needed, but any interruption would be welcome. Almost any. His gaze locked onto Lauren's. No way. Anyone but her at this moment. Tori came in right behind her, her eyes widening at the sight of Bailey and Skylar invading James's and Kade's space.

Lauren pivoted on her heel, but Tori blocked the escape.

That's when James noticed the slim black capris and long, soft-looking tunic — nothing like he'd ever seen on

Lauren before. Her hair was different, too. The curls swished as she shook her head emphatically at Tori. James swallowed hard. Lauren looked... well, there wasn't any other word for it. She looked hot. To say nothing of hot under the collar.

"Hey, Tori, Lauren," Kade said easily. "Abigail just put on another pot of coffee. Pull up a chair."

If Bailey leaned any harder, she'd push James off his seat. It would make a scene, but it might not be a bad way to go. At least Lauren would know this wasn't his idea.

Wait a sec. Tori. She'd told him not to give up on Lauren. Was she responsible for Lauren's transformation? For them both arriving at Java Springs right now? He'd mentioned over lunch that he was meeting Kade for coffee. Yeah, his sister had set this up. Big question was, had she dropped a clue to Bailey and Skylar? She wouldn't have stooped that low, would she?

He raised his eyebrows at his sister and barely caught the twitch of her shoulders and the tiny shake of her head.

"I just remembered I have a patient coming at three-thirty." Lauren pushed at Tori.

His sister didn't move. "Then you're so late they've already left. Come on. I'm dying for a coffee."

"Strawberry muffins just came out of the oven," sang out Abigail.

"Yum!" Tori grasped Lauren's arm and towed her to the two vacant chairs across from James and Kade. The ones Bailey and Skylar might have grabbed if they weren't so busy trying to touch men they had no business touching.

"Hey, Lauren," Kade said conversationally. "How are things? I haven't seen you in a while."

"That can only be good news, right?" Tori beamed. "That means all the animals at Eaglecrest are healthy."

"What on earth are you talking about?" demanded Bailey.

"Oh, hi, Bailey. I didn't see you there."

Touché. At least Tori's words made the brazen woman pull back a little.

"This is my friend, Dr. Yanovich, the owner of Saddle Springs Veterinary Clinic."

"Co-owner." Lauren straightened her shoulders slightly as she took the seat across from Kade.

"Bailey and Skylar are at the ranch for a quick visit." Tori swept her hand as though it were of no consequence. "They work in an office in Chicago."

How to downplay it. James cheered inwardly.

Bailey's hand rested on James's shoulder. "We're thinking of relocating."

LAUREN YANKED out of the wooden chair and strode to the counter at the back where Abigail Evening set a platter of muffins in the display case.

"I'll take a caramel macchiato to go, Abigail. Triple shot." Yeah, her nerves were already strung to the max. There wasn't much the extra jolt of caffeine could do to her. Probably. She looked back to the table as the woman who'd been draped over Kade settled into the chair she'd just vacated. James's new love interest stayed where she was, touching him, but smiling at Lauren, her eyes wide.

Hussy.

If this was how James wanted to move on, more power to him. She hadn't bought this outfit for him, anyway. She'd bought it because Denae had hauled nearly everything in her closet out to the curb in a trash bag. And Denae had been correct. This had nothing to do with James. Lauren had told him to date other women, had tried to set him up. She'd told him no when he'd sort of kind of proposed, so how could she complain when he finally got the hint?

She pasted on a bright smile and turned back to Abigail. "I'd love a couple of those muffins, too." She'd better not eat too many or she wouldn't fit her new wardrobe for long, but today was for indulging. She'd probably expend all the calories in a crying jag anyway. Hopefully she'd make it home before the floodgates burst. Why had they walked, anyway?

"I'll take a vanilla latte to go," Tori said from beside Lauren.

"Oh, you don't have to leave just because I do."

"Of course, I do. Friends don't let friends caffeinate alone."

In a heartbeat, Lauren was turning sixteen on a raft on a small lake, surrounded by the gang and a cute guy who just so happened to share her birthday. *Friends don't let friends turn thirty... single.*

Oh, man. Those tears were about to gush. She'd been so innocent then. Crushed because Dillon had broken up with her when she should never have been stupid enough to date the moron in the first place. If only she could tell Past Lauren to save her tears for when they really mattered, and never, ever high-five on something important.

The middle-aged barista set the to-go cup on the counter and snapped the lid tight. "Here you go, hon. I'll do up Tori's drink and then box up some muffins for you both."

"What do we have to do to get some coffee around here?" whined one of the women.

Kade laughed. "You order it at the counter and pay for it, just like every coffee shop I've ever been in. Is it different in Chicago?"

Silence.

Lauren would not turn and look. Definitely not. She would stare at Abigail's back as she prepped Tori's drink then tap her card and be gone. She might or might not sneak a quick peek at James on her way past.

A couple of minutes later she emerged into the cloudy June afternoon, Tori at her heels. When the door had clicked shut behind them, Lauren whirled on her friend. "You knew. You did that on purpose. You told me to change before we went out for coffee."

Tori winced, hands full.

Lauren wasn't done. "I trusted you and Denae. She's probably in on it, too."

"Calm down." The flick in Tori's eyes assured Lauren she was right.

"Calm *down*? After that display of... of *lust*?"

Tori nudged her to start walking down Main Street. "Yes, calm down. Bailey, Skylar, and their friend are on an unfortunate mission. I'd like to point out that I had no idea they'd be there, and James looked super uncomfortable."

"Because he'd been caught."

"Hey. That's my brother you're talking about, and you know better." Steel fortified Tori's words.

Lauren whirled, her elbow catching Tori's arm. "Of course, you're on his side."

"Listen to yourself. If that's not jealousy talking, the world is silent."

"I'm not jealous. If that's how he wants to play it, it's his life. Go ahead."

Tori's eyebrows rose.

"Seriously. What have I been saying all along? I'm perfectly happy being single. My career gives me a full life. I live to ease the suffering of animals, teach the little ones in Sunday School — thanks for filling in, by the way — and enjoying the beauty of God's creation here on the edge of the mountains. What more do I need?"

"And what of the confession that night on the mountaintop?"

Lauren shrugged, waving a hand. "A moment of weakness. I'm over it."

"It's okay to be honest," Tori said softly.

Nope. Not with James's sister. Look where that had gotten her. Lauren marched up the street, holding her to-go cup in front of her like a sword. If she could only get rid of Tori, but her friend's vehicle was parked in front of the duplex. Plus, she needed those muffins. Nah, they were too healthy. What she really needed was Häagen-Dazs, and there happened to be a pint of chocolate salted fudge truffle in her freezer right now. Tori could have the strawberry muffins.

Tori made a couple of additional attempts at conversation as they all but jogged the few blocks back to Lauren's. Just a few yards to solitude, Lauren sped up. She'd get inside and bolt the door on Tori. Cry now, explain later if she had to, but she couldn't — just couldn't — deal with Tori right now. She'd probably report right back to James.

Denae crossed the porch of the duplex to Lauren's door, a wide grin on her face. "Did you two have fun?"

Lauren skidded to a stop. "You, too?" she spat out.

Denae's smile faltered. "Uh oh."

"Bailey got there first, and she was all draped over James's shoulder when we walked in." Tori's voice was tinged with regret.

How was it even possible to be angrier than she'd been a minute ago? But Lauren was absolutely seeing red, with blood pulsing in her temples. "Nice. And I thought you were my friends."

Tori sighed. "We are."

"Right. Friends don't sneak around people's backs and try to maneuver things."

"Not as a rule," said Tori. "Only when their friend is unusually stubborn."

Lauren rolled her eyes. "Get a life and do it elsewhere." She considered Denae, who blocked her door, and took a deep, shuddering breath. Her head pounded, and the geyser of tears was imminent. "Please leave me alone."

"You can't have it both ways, Lauren."

She pivoted back to Tori. "What exactly are you trying to say?"

"Friendship according to Lauren. Friends do this, friends don't do that. You know what? Friends are people, too. We mess up, all of us. We're human. You can't blame me for wanting you and my brother to be happy. You can't blame me for Bailey's actions, and you can't blame James, either. That woman has been pursuing him for a week, pulling out all the stops, but he's managed to evade her. He and Matt are sticking together like burrs every day so she can't get one of them alone. Do you have any idea how many riding lessons I've given those bimbos because I'm the only one they won't chase? When they figured out they couldn't get to James that way, they quit wanting lessons and they just hang around the stables all the livelong day. Mom is *this* close to kicking them off the ranch, but offering a refund grates hard, so we're all just trying to survive the next week. What do you think of that?"

Lauren took a step back. "I didn't know."

"You didn't know because you're stuck in Lauren Land. If you'd get off your high horse and actually look around, you'd know there was more to Saddle Springs than poor you. I'm done. I can't remember why I wanted you for a sister-in-law." She shoved the box of muffins at Lauren. "Here. I don't want them." The click of her cowboy boots was the only sound as she strode to the Flying Horseshoe pickup and hopped in. Then the truck roared down the street.

"Wow," breathed Denae.

The tears leaked out now. Lauren's lip trembled. She pushed the box at Denae. "Here, have some muffins."

"Are they low-fat?"

"Who stinking cares about calories?"

Denae's eyes narrowed as she crossed her arms in front of her. She was so skinny there was nothing to cover. "Some of us do."

Lauren reached for the trash can which, just last week, had been stuffed with her sweats, and dumped the box inside. She could sure use those comfort clothes now. All of them. The money she'd spent on a new wardrobe was a total waste. No veterinarian without a social life needed swishy dresses and tailored tops and fitted pants. Not over a thousand dollars' worth.

She pushed past Denae, entered her haven, and twisted the lock behind her. Felix twined around her ankles, and she scooped him up on her way to the freezer.

Chapter 17

James pushed Jigsaw into a ground-eating canter. The two of them hadn't felt the wind on their faces since the trail ride. Not even really then, with the packhorses on their leads and the group around them.

Lauren.

Oh, God. How could things have gone from cautiously hopeful to full-on fury in just a few short weeks? Why had Bailey and Skylar chosen that exact moment to enter the coffee shop? Why had his *darling* sister decided to interfere? Oh, yeah, Tori was full of tears and apologies when they were back at the Flying Horseshoe, but that didn't help, did it? Nope.

He lifted his eyes to the mountains soaring above the trees along the trail. "God, what are You doing? Anything? Don't You even care?"

Jigsaw's ears flicked at James's shout, but she was too well trained to let her pace falter.

What is man that You are mindful of him, and the son of man that You care for him? Yet You have made him a little lower than the heavenly beings and crowned him with glory and honor.

The words from Psalm eight pulsed through his mind. They ended with, *O Lord, our Lord, how majestic is Your name in all the earth*. Words he'd sung just last Sunday when he and Garret had led worship.

He was a farce. He didn't deserve to stand up front and lead anyone anywhere. Not with his heart in turmoil.

Do you trust Me?

That was the big question, wasn't it? Oh, James knew he should. It was a direct order in the Bible: *trust in the Lord with all your heart, and lean not on your own understanding. In all your ways, submit to Him, and He will make your paths straight.* Proverbs 3:5-6 had been drilled into his head since he was a little kid like Aiden in Sunday School.

James drifted back to Pastor Roland's sermon series a while back, the one about knowing God's will. He'd been so sure then that he was on the right track. He'd claimed verses like Psalm 37:4, where it said, *delight yourself in the Lord, and He will give you the desires of your heart.* Wasn't that whole chapter about focusing on God in the face of evildoers? Bailey definitely qualified. And the desire of James's heart? Lauren.

Heels down, he shifted in the saddle as Jigsaw settled into a trot. Pines and aspens swept by. One of the creeks feeding the ranch's small lake gurgled beside the trail. The clouds had drifted apart, allowing sunshine to angle into the deep gully, and a gentle breeze freshened the air and caressed his face.

Was his heart's desire really Lauren? He was pretty sure that wasn't what the psalmist meant. There'd been a brief discussion in the church's Facebook group when someone listed that verse as a biblical reference to God's will. Pastor Roland reminded them that when folks truly focused on delighting in the Lord, they were incapable of holding hearts' desires that weren't in line with scripture.

That whole sermon series had both comforted and confused James. He wanted God's will. He truly did. But it seemed vague and spiritual, not at all practical. He wanted God to point to Lauren and declare in a booming voice loud enough for both of them to hear, "you two are meant for each other."

But Pastor Roland had made a good point that such a narrow view of God's will faltered with any wrong decision, no matter how small. Maybe God hadn't meant for him to meet Kade at Java Springs this afternoon. Had he prayed about it? No. At his buddy's call, he'd grabbed the blueprints and headed to town, thankful for a sympathetic, experienced friend to help him make decisions about the house. Did God care if he ordered the oak or hickory cabinets? Could a person actually pray about every single choice?

Well, yeah, the Bible said to pray without ceasing, but about what? Whether the bathroom sink was vessel or inset? If not, when did a decision become life-changing enough to be worth talking to God about? Surely a marriage partner fit that category. That would impact his life every day in every way, unlike the choice between backsplash tiles.

James lifted his gaze to the mountains, where the morning shower in the valley had dusted the soaring peaks with light snow. Everything seemed in such a turmoil. How could a guy step back in the midst of it all and get his bearings again?

Do you love Me?

"You know I do, Lord." Reminiscent of Peter, but Jesus had called the apostle to feed His sheep and grow His church. Peter had heard what God's will for him was in those words. Were those words for James, too? Was ministry God's will for him?

He honestly didn't think so. He tightened his knees on Jigsaw's sides, and the mare picked up her pace again. The Flying Horseshoe was all he'd ever wanted. Riding and helping others see the beauty of God's creation in a new way. Pastor Roland and the members of Springs of Living Water Church appreciated James's leadership and his gift of music. He dug into the Word, participated in group Bible studies, and joined his buddies in Cowboy Santa, where they'd shown Jesus' love to a bunch of needy families just a few months back.

No, James was pretty sure he was right where God wanted him. The only hole in his life and heart was a wife, a family. He longed for Lauren, but somehow their relationship had gone from best friends to awkwardness to rejection to anger. Now what? Was redemption even possible from here?

Trust in the Lord with all your heart, and lean not on your own understanding. In all your ways, submit to Him, and He will make your paths straight. In *all* your ways. Yes, God did care about the details.

James understood what Pastor Roland had been trying to say, that a guy shouldn't get so worried about the details that he forgot the bigger picture, where he needed to delight and trust in the Lord. But that didn't mean God didn't have a plan for James's life. He'd just been going about searching for it from the wrong angle. From now on, he was going to forget about that upcoming thirtieth birthday and focus on strengthening his relationship with the Lord.

With a lighter heart, he turned Jigsaw toward home.

LAUREN THREW herself into her work. She'd disinfected all the kennels — again — cleaned all the drawers and cabinets in her office and dropped by the nearby ranches to check on past patients. Well, most of the ranches. She stayed clear of the Flying Horseshoe and all of the Delgado family holdings because of Kade's close friendship with James. She'd managed to avoid her mother, her tenant, and James's sister all week by turning off the ringer on her phone, managing her time creatively, and leaving her Jeep parked at the clinic so it was less obvious when she was home. The few blocks' walk canceled living on frozen pizza and ice cream, right?

How long could she go on like this? It had been a lonely week for a woman who thrived in the presence of friends, but her friends weren't to be trusted. Maybe she needed new ones, but that would mean changing churches and cutting all ties. That seemed a bit extreme.

She had choices to make. She could sell her duplex and her half of the practice and leave Saddle Springs in the dust. Neither would happen overnight. She could quit going to church and keep hiding, but how long could that last? Or she could deal with it. Stick her chin up, pull on those big-girl panties, and get over herself. Get over James.

It was Saturday. Tori had filled in for her teaching the toddler Sunday school class the past two weeks. Phoning and asking for a third Sunday was not an option, especially since she wasn't speaking to Tori. And if she *was* talking to James's sister, she was halfway to Option Three. Some days, being a responsible adult was annoying.

Lauren sighed and tightened her hands on the Jeep's steering wheel. She'd pointed the SUV toward Missoula from a need to escape. All the busy work this week hadn't helped, nor had wandering Jacobs Island Park. She still saw that bombshell in her tight shorts and even tighter camisole draped over James's shoulder. Granted, he hadn't been hugging her back, but he also hadn't pushed her away. He'd stared at Lauren rather thunderstruck, like he couldn't believe he'd been caught. Had they done all their kissing at the Flying Horseshoe before and after?

Tori could probably fill her in, but Lauren wouldn't ask. She was done, done, done.

Which, she supposed, answered her question. Tomorrow morning she'd show up at church, at least long enough to teach Sunday school. She'd take the high road and pretend seeing James and what's-her-face in the coffee shop hadn't yanked the rug out from beneath her. The silly thing was she'd been pushing him to date someone else for a couple of years. Why did it hurt like a knife in the chest when he finally took her up on it? He'd asked her to marry him — yes, out of duty, but he'd done it — she'd said no, and he was moving on.

This was what she wanted. So, yes, she'd start acting like an adult again, but tomorrow was soon enough. Tonight, she'd hit the drive-through on her way back to Saddle Springs and indulge in a greasy double cheeseburger, salty fries, and a mega-size milkshake for the road.

"What's going on with Lauren?" Meg asked over Sunday lunch. "Tori, do you know? You've subbed for her a lot recently. She was teaching today but seemed too busy to chat when I picked up Aiden, and then I didn't see her in the service."

James reached for his mom's pasta salad, aware of Tori's quick glance.

"Um..."

Wow, Tori was eloquent for someone who knew far too much. Dad knew, so Mom probably did, too. He should never have let his little sister push him into confiding. That only left Meg and Eli, so what was the point? James sighed. "She's mad at me."

"At you?" Meg tapped James's hand with the sausage

tongs. "What's going on here? I thought you two were besties."

James breathed a prayer. In his quest to deepen his relationship with Jesus, he'd decided to quit dodging and hiding. Now he was faced with the reality. "It's a long story," he warned. "Starts when we were teenagers."

Meg and Eli exchanged glances. "She hasn't been mad at you *that* long."

"No, you're right. I'm going to tell you, but this is in confidence, okay?" The teenage Meg could never have been trusted not to blab, but she'd matured a lot since Aiden's birth. Eli, too, had been good for her. And, well, she was his sister.

"Okay. Sure." Meg raised her eyebrows at him and settled both hands on her round stomach. "Spill the deets."

He gave the short version, wishing he could gloss over the trail ride and then over Bailey's part in the story, especially. Then he took a bite of pasta salad.

Meg shook her head. "Where's the part where you kissed her passionately and told her you loved her?"

James choked on his bite. "In your imagination." And in his.

"No, seriously. You're an idiot."

"That's what I told him," Tori put in. "What do you think, Mom?"

"Well, your father mentioned a bit of this a few weeks ago. And we did know those girls from Chicago were causing problems, but not off the property. Did they follow you to town, Jamie?"

He shook his head. "Not as far as I know. I think it was just accidentally bad timing. Unless Tori thought she'd be helpful and set me up." For a fall.

"I would never!"

James shrugged. "The thought crossed my mind. It seemed all too convenient."

Tori stabbed at the salad on her plate. "I admit to knowing you'd be there and dragging Lauren in. But I had no clue Bailey and Skylar were downtown. Trust me."

"So, you were interfering?" Disapproval colored Mom's voice.

"Don't start, Mom. I've always liked Lauren and thought she and James would eventually figure out they're in love. I was just giving things a little nudge. Yes, it was a bad idea. I'm sorry, okay? I didn't expect the universe to blow up."

"What are you going to do now?" Meg cut Aiden's sausage into smaller pieces.

"I've spent a lot of time praying since it happened," James admitted. "I discovered I haven't been trusting the Lord with my future. I've been leaning on my own understanding instead, and it's been faulty. So, I'm not sure what my next step will be. I'm trying to be patient and submit to God's will."

"Or you could try kissing her." Meg sounded exasperated.

The thought had definitely crossed James's mind. He shrugged and glanced at his father.

Dad's eyes twinkled. "Kissing definitely has its place. It's a wonderful part of making up after a fight."

A squeaky sound came from Mom.

He slipped his arm around the back of her chair. "Pretty sure the kids know we've had an argument or two over the years, Amanda. And I know they've seen us kissing." Dad turned his attention back to James. "But I agree with you, son. You've been unsettled for months but, in the past few days, I've noticed a change in you. Keep seeking the Lord, and He *will* reveal Himself to you. It sounds like Lauren hasn't yet come to that realization, and we can't do it for someone else, no matter how good our intentions." He looked around at the family. "We will all pray for you both, that God's will becomes clear."

"One more thing." Mom stared at Tori. "Look up First Thessalonians four verses eleven and twelve. You might want to meditate on that whole section, since it fits very well into Pastor Roland's sermon series about God's will."

Tori let out a long breath and a guilty look. "Yes, Mom."

Chapter 18

Lauren sat back on her heels beside the litter of newborn Border Collie puppies.

The dogs' owner knelt beside her. "I'm a bit worried about this one." Carmen Haviland picked up the tiny black-and-white runt and cradled it.

"She seems listless." Lauren stroked the little head with a finger. No reaction. "Her vitals are in range, though. And she's not much smaller than the others."

"I've got a bad feeling." Carmen tucked the pup in place at Selah's side, where the littermates eagerly rooted for milk. The runt didn't participate. "Should I try supplementing her?"

"You could. We have bottles and canine milk replacer at the clinic." Lauren should have thought to put some in the Jeep, just in case, though there'd been nothing to indicate this wouldn't be a routine newborn checkup. "Tuck Morrison is waiting on me to check out a lame horse, but I can run some out later, if you like."

Carmen shook her head. "I can't afford to pay you for an extra trip. If the pup isn't thriving by morning, I'll stop by when I'm in town anyway."

"I won't charge you." Lauren knew how hard her friend worked, trying to get a dog breeding and training business going. Carmen had been struggling ever since her husband's death a few years ago, trying to convince Eric's great uncle, owner of the Rocking H, that she should inherit the ranch when the old man passed on. Eric had been Howard's heir, after all, and their daughter had been born right on the property.

"I'm not asking for charity."

Lauren elbowed her friend lightly. "I'm not offering it."

Carmen sighed. "Don't worry about it. Everything will be fine, I'm sure. I'll be solvent — or at least a lot closer — when all Gwynn's puppies are paid for and picked up. They're almost ready for their owners... and then there is this batch of Selah's. I'd hoped for more than four pups." Her gaze slid to the runt.

So did Lauren's. "She'll probably be just fine."

"Yeah. I can't help worrying some." Carmen pulled to her feet. "I'll keep a close eye on them all and let you know if anything changes. Right now, keeping Juliana out of here is one of my biggest concerns. You'd think she'd be more excited about playing with Gwynn's pups since they can run with her now, but Selah is her favorite."

"They should be handled as little as possible for the first few weeks."

"I know, and I've told Juliana repeatedly. I really need

to make this breeding business work, and I've got a couple of one-year-olds coming this fall for sheep-dog training. Now, if only I could convince Uncle Howard this is a legitimate sideline for the Rocking H."

"He's old-school. Ranches mean horses and cows, not dog training, especially for sheep."

"They herd cows, too." Carmen raised both hands. "I know, I know. I've probably killed any hope of making Howard reconsider. It's just that I love this place and so does Juliana. I don't want to raise her anywhere else, and without Eric's inheritance, I certainly can't afford my own acreage to run sheep and dogs."

Lauren had been dying of curiosity ever since the old man's will had become public knowledge. "Why is he giving everything to the other great-nephew? I don't even know if I've ever met Spencer."

"Ranching is macho man's business, not for weak females."

They rolled their eyes at the same time then laughed.

Carmen sobered first. "You and I both know the main thing about keeping a ranch in the black is good management. I can hire someone for the brute labor, but Howard doesn't see it that way. To him, being a rancher is all about riding the range and doing everything himself. A loner."

"And that's why the Rocking H has declined since he got too old to handle things."

"You're not telling me anything I don't know, but try to convince him. What a joke."

"Maybe you can make a deal with Spencer. Is he a reasonable kind of guy?"

Carmen sucked in her lower lip. "I have no clue, but I doubt it. He's worked in an accounting firm in Dallas forever. I've seen him twice in the past few years — at our wedding, and at Eric's funeral."

"I don't get why Howard thinks someone who never visits would be best for the ranch. Does Spencer even want it?"

"Time will tell, I guess." Carmen turned and watched the puppies. "Meanwhile, I have to do what I can to get in Howard's good graces and convince him I have a solid plan."

"Or maybe you should forget the Rocking H and start looking for a husband." Lauren was done pushing women at James. The guy had made his decision, and Bailey wasn't the sort of person she'd wish on anyone. "There are several ranchers' sons in the area. Oh, I know! How about Trevor Delgado? Standing Rock Ranch has plenty of room for you, Juliana, the sheep, and the dogs."

"Are you crazy?" Carmen's eyebrows shot up. "Definitely not Trevor. And don't even suggest Sawyer."

"I wasn't going to." The youngest Delgado brother was in competition, same as Carmen's deceased husband, who'd died after being gored by a bull. Lauren could see why Carmen wouldn't be interested in a rodeo cowboy again. "There's Bryce Sutherland down south of town. He's a pretty nice guy."

"Lauren?"

"Hmm?"

"I mean this in the nicest possible way, but stop it, okay? If I'm going to remarry, I'll find the guy myself."

"I was just trying to help."

"Well, don't."

Nobody seemed to appreciate the fact that Lauren knew all the ranchers in the area and probably two-thirds of the rest of Saddle Springs' population. The veterinary clinic treated everyone's pets and stock. Well, fine. It was no skin off her back if her friends didn't appreciate a tip here and there.

Just stop. James's words. Kade had said the same last summer, and Trevor only raised his eyebrows at her suggestions for him. Garret was the only one who looked remotely thoughtful, but that didn't mean he was taking her any more seriously than the other guys.

She forced a smile even as her gut roiled. "I need to get down to Canyon Crossing. Let me know how things go with the puppy."

"I will." Carmen fell into step beside her as they walked out to the Jeep. "Sorry if I came across as offensive. That wasn't my intention."

"No problem. Sorry for interfering." Lauren climbed into her vehicle. "Talk to you later."

"Hey, can you watch Aiden?" Eli appeared at the round corral where James worked with Snowball. "Meg's gone into labor, and I can't find your mom anywhere."

James blinked to attention and gave a gentle tug on the lunge line. "Halt."

Snowball broke her stride, watching him closely, then came to a stop, tossing her head. He moved toward the mare, gathering the line in large loops before running his hands over her head and whispering sweet nothings in her flickering ear. Then he tugged her halter as he crossed the dusty corral to where his brother-in-law stood, bracing Aiden on the top rail.

"She's a beauty," Eli said. "Rosebud doing okay?"

James nodded, still stroking Snowball's neck. "They're both doing well, and this way Mama gets a bit of exercise and doesn't forget all her training." He tipped his hat back and eyed his brother-in-law. "Isn't this early for Meg?"

"Only a couple of weeks. Last time we were in, Doc said she wasn't far off. Anyway, I hate to ask you when I can see you're busy."

"But Tori's on a trail ride with guests, and Mom's in a meeting with Ollie about the Fourth of July menu." James chucked his nephew's chin. "This little dude can hang out with Uncle James anytime."

"Thanks." Eli's expression relaxed. "I owe you one."

James shook his head. "No, you don't. Family is family. C'mere, Aiden. Want to see the foal?"

Aiden flung himself off the corral rail with a squeal and nearly strangled James with two short, tight arms around his throat. "Bye, Daddy."

Eli chuckled. "All right, then. Got your phone on you? In case I need to get in touch?"

James patted his snapped-down shirt pocket as he shifted Aiden to a more comfortable position. "Yep, right here. Tell Meg I'm praying for her, okay?"

"Thanks, man." Eli turned and strode toward the ranch ATV he'd driven over from their house.

Things were sure different from Aiden's birth. Meg was different. Grown up, in love, giving of herself to others instead of the selfish, willful person she'd been. She credited it all to God whopping her upside the head when she found herself pregnant and alone. While it was hard to argue all her difficulties had been God's will, the result had been a woman whose life had completely reversed direction.

"Unca James!" Aiden bounced on his arm as the ATV roared away. "Pet horsey?"

"Be gentle." James turned so the child could hug Snowball's large head. "You have to listen really good, okay?"

"Okay."

James kept his nephew within arm's reach and made an attempt to do some of his chores. A three-year-old sure kept a guy on his toes.

"James?" His mom's voice came from nearby. "Heard anything from Eli? And hello there, Nanna's favorite little cowpoke."

Aiden squealed and scrambled off the corral fence where James had parked him. Mom scooped him up.

James pushed his cowboy hat higher on his forehead. "He sent you a message earlier, right?"

"Two. One asking if I could take Aiden then another saying you had him. Nothing since."

"Me, either." James tugged out his phone and checked, but he had not missed the ding of an incoming message. "It's been only an hour or two. I guess it takes longer for a human to give birth than a horse."

Mom laughed. "Yes. Yes, it does. Odds are she's just getting started." She squeezed Aiden and gave him a twirl. The little guy chortled.

James's heart pinched. Would he ever have a son like Aiden or a daughter like the infant his sister was struggling to birth right now? Would his mom ever blow raspberries on his children's throats and hear them giggle in response?

Could he really get over Lauren and then date and marry someone else? Only in theory. In practice, he'd been tuned to her for half his life, and moving on was not in his agenda.

Maybe his sisters were right. Maybe he should simply walk up to Lauren and kiss her like he meant it... because he did. Maybe he'd muddled things on the trail ride. Never mind the maybe. Somehow, she'd felt like a pity project, something that had never occurred to him. He'd only been trying to explain the progression in his head.

He loved her. She might be focused and opinionated, but so was he. It could all be channeled for good, couldn't it? If she ever let him get within ten feet of her again.

"You okay, Jamie?" Mom's eyebrows furrowed as she watched him over Aiden's shoulder. "Megan will be fine."

"It's not Meg."

"Lauren?"

James nodded. "I know I should just let it all rest in God's hands, but it's hard."

Mom slipped an arm around his waist, and Aiden flung himself at James. "Your dad and I are praying for you both."

Aiden burbled a kiss against James's scruffy cheeks then giggled until it turned into a belly laugh. It was impossible to stay serious with the little clown in his arms. Aiden's laughter was simply infectious. James rubbed his whiskers gently over his nephew's soft cheek, and the little guy shrieked in delight.

"Thanks, Mom. I can't tell you how much I appreciate your support."

"It will work out. God's got it."

She sounded so serene. Was it just because it wasn't her life in turmoil? No. She'd held on to God's sovereignty as far back as James could remember, even through the horrible accident that nearly took Dad's life and left him crippled. If Mom had ever had doubts, she'd poured them out to God, not in front of her children. Her words weren't sweet, untested platitudes, but a result of deep, enduring faith.

James needed to do the same. Pour out everything to the Lord and stop whining to his family and friends about how Lauren misunderstood his feeble proclamation. Grow some faith. Live by God's will as revealed in Scripture. The list on the church Facebook group continued to grow, weeks later. He'd started taking one of the references every morning and meditating on it, asking God to help him put it into practice.

Mom's phone rang, and she pulled it out. "It's Eli," she told James as she tapped to accept. "Hello? ... Taking her to Missoula? ... Is everything okay? ... Yes, Aiden's fine. He can stay with us, no problem ... Take care of our girls ... Love you, too. We'll keep praying." She took a deep breath and turned to James. "The baby's in distress. They're sending Meg to Missoula for a C-section."

Mustang County Hospital wasn't equipped to handle anything out of the ordinary, but James still hadn't expected his niece to be born outside of Saddle Springs. He wrapped one arm around his mom's shoulders. "And so we pray."

Pray for God's will to be done. Wasn't that getting to be the story of his life?

Chapter 19

Lauren curled up in her bed, Felix tucked against her, and stared at her Bible reading app. The thing was programmed to tell it like it was, right? Could she really have missed this many days of digging into God's word? One more layer of guilt piled onto the others. She was a failure at everything. She was a lousy daughter and a terrible friend. She wasn't even a very good veterinarian. How could that pup of Carmen's go from listless to lifeless in under eighteen hours? It wasn't just that Carmen couldn't afford the loss, but that Lauren had gotten busy — or call it distracted — and hadn't driven back to the Rocking H with puppy formula. She hadn't checked back. She *always* checked back.

She sighed as she glanced over the chapter for the next reading. Seriously? Ezekiel forty-one was all about the prophet's vision for a new temple, when Israel's reality was captivity in Babylon. She'd think the guy was an optimist if she hadn't already read the earlier chapters and found all the dire warnings he'd given his people and the surrounding nations. Being a prophet must've been a nasty job. No one liked a naysayer.

Fact was, Lauren wasn't in the mood for Ezekiel's woes. She had enough of her own, thanks. She'd missed so many days now — what was one more? She flicked her phone over to Facebook, and the church group's discussion about God's will popped to the top of her newsfeed. She'd call catching up on that her devotional time.

The last entry was Tori Carmichael with First Thessalonians 4:11-12: *Make it your ambition to lead a quiet life: You should mind your own business and work with your hands, just as we told you, so that your daily life may win the respect of outsiders and so that you will not be dependent on anybody.*

She stared at the words. *Mind your own business.*

Ouch. She'd been trying to help her friends, hadn't she? No, not really. She'd been focused on trying to get James permanently off her heart and mind. All the other matchmaking had been to deflect attention off her top priority. Not only had it not worked, she'd sinned by doing it. It hadn't seemed so bad, especially not at first.

Lauren scanned the rest of the group's new additions to the thread. Psalm 96:2: *Sing to the Lord, praise His name; proclaim His salvation day after day.* 2 Peter 1:5-8: *Make every effort to add to your faith goodness; and to goodness, knowledge; and to knowledge, self-control; and to self-control, perseverance; and to perseverance, godliness; and to godliness, mutual affection; and to mutual affection, love. For if you possess these qualities in increasing measure, they will keep you from being ineffective and unproductive in your knowledge of our Lord Jesus Christ.*

There were more additions to the list. Good verses that reminded her to focus on godly attributes. To focus on God Himself and on being an effective, productive Christian. Not focusing on her own woes — some days, it felt like she could write a book to rival Ezekiel's — but on growth through the trials. Keeping her own heart riveted on Jesus.

Her gaze slid back to Tori's entry. *My mom drew my attention to these verses as a reminder to focus on my own growth and not worry about how everyone else is doing. I wrote them on a notecard and stuck it to my bathroom mirror, so I'd see it often. I hope it challenges you as much as it did me.*

Tears smarted in Lauren's eyes. Why had Amanda Carmichael felt the need to share this scripture with her daughter? Was it Lauren's fault, leading Tori astray? "Really, God. I didn't mean to. What do I do now?"

Repent, my beloved.

Repent. Didn't that mean to be sorry then do a one-eighty? "I'm sorry," she whispered. But for what, exactly? Her eyes went back to the verse. "I'm sorry for not minding my own business. Lord, I'm sorry for trying to direct the lives of others. I'm sorry for losing my way."

The lightening in her spirit told her she was on the right path now. "I'm sorry for thinking I knew more than You did about what's best for others. Even thinking that about myself."

Tears began to stream. Felix reached up and patted her cheek with his paw, and she clutched him to her chest. "Oh, kitty. I've made such a mess."

A suspicion fell over her that repenting to God was

not the only requirement. She'd wronged people, too. Tori. Denae. Carmen. James. Especially James.

Lauren tilted her gaze to the ceiling. "God, do I really have to apologize to James? That will open this whole mess back up again, and he'll feel obligated to repeat that awkward proposal. I love him, Lord, but I can't stand the thought of being married to him if he doesn't love me back."

Of course, God loved the church as though she were a holy bride, and the church wasn't exactly full of passion back. Did that mean a one-sided love, paired with reasonable affection, could be enough? She was pretty sure James *liked* her okay. Maybe, in time, he'd come to truly love her as she longed to be loved.

But, what if he didn't? It would be even worse if she accepted his proposal, poured out her heart's desire, and he remained dutiful and honorable. Her heart would shrivel up and die.

Trust Me, my child.

Yeah, God had a lot of experience with that. Of putting Himself on the line, literally, and being rejected outright or only partially accepted. But could she truly trust Him to walk her through this difficult, painful time? Was her faith so weak? It would likely be stronger if she hadn't skipped her devotions so many days. Another thing to repent of and turn away from.

But, for now, she slowly stretched her hand into the air and visualized placing it in the hand of her Savior. "I trust You, Jesus. Help me know how and when to make my apology. I've got to admit, I'm shaking to the bottoms of my feet about this whole thing, so please prepare James as well as me."

There's no time like the present.

Lauren winced and glanced at her bedside clock. It was only nine o'clock. Dusk but not dark, and definitely not too late to drive out to the Flying Horseshoe. James would be done with his work for the day and likely be in his cabin.

Besides, how would she ever sleep with this hanging over her? Probably better to get it over with. Now, what should she wear?

***

JAMES SAT out on his back deck and put his feet on the railing, watching the last rays of sunlight flicker across the surface of the small lake. He'd miss this at the new house. Oh, he'd have a better view of the setting sun through the gap in the mountains, but the lake wouldn't be part of the vista. He could catch sunrises on the lake, instead. At least some days.

Life seemed more full of sunsets than sunrises. How was that for doom-and-gloom thinking for a guy who'd be thirty in three short weeks? He pushed the thought aside as blaring music from the cabin next door cut in half with the slide of their patio door. A child cried from a cabin further down. A vehicle pulled into the parking area. Doors slammed. More voices.

Yeah, being a bit farther from the center of all the action would be nice. He could always go inside — the cabin's timber walls cut virtually all the sounds of the guest ranch — but he hated to miss winding down with a view of nature.

The random noise, though, he could do something about. He tugged his buds from a shirt pocket and plugged them into his phone then into his ears, selecting a medley of instrumental worship music at a low volume.

There. Much better. He hunkered back down into his deck chair and let the familiar melodies wash over his spirit.

Mom and Dad had taken Aiden to Missoula to see Meg, Eli, and little Sophia Grace, who was no worse off for the dramatic entrance she'd made. They'd be back in Saddle Springs in a few days, and James would have his chance to meet his tiny niece. Mom had shown him about thirty photos on her phone, and the one he'd stared at the longest was Eli cradling the infant.

James closed his eyes, remembering the besotted expression on his brother-in-law's face. The guy practically glowed. He'd had an experience — spiritual as well as physical — that James longed for. No matter how much James prayed for God to remove his love for Lauren, she continued to invade every waking moment and half his sleeping ones. How long would it take? Could he keep doing this? What choice did he have?

The sun disappeared behind the peaks, the shimmering path fading on the lake. Dots of light from the cabins reflected on the water. An owl whooshed past, so close James could probably have touched it.

His phone rang, the thrum interrupting the flowing

music. Unknown number, but that wasn't shocking. His mom had probably forgotten to turn off call forwarding when they returned from Missoula. It was likely a reservation.

"Flying Horseshoe Guest Ranch, James Carmichael speaking." He'd probably need a pen and notepad to record the information, but he wouldn't move until he had to.

"James?" A familiar female voice giggled.

His eyes shot open and his feet hit the planks of the deck as he jerked upright. No way.

"Listen, it's Bailey Gabriel. Remember me?"

"Uh, yes?" He kept his voice guarded. What on earth could she want? It had been a peaceful week since she and her friends had returned to Chicago.

"This is awkward." She giggled again.

He couldn't think of any response, so he simply waited.

"Look, I just wanted to say I'm sorry. I was a bit of a jerk when we were in Montana."

James held the phone out and looked at it. Was this real or a prank call? Was she high on something right now? Because she'd been more than a jerk.

"Say something. You're making me nervous."

"Uh, apology accepted." So long as she didn't think that meant he wanted a relationship with her. Nothing could be farther from the truth.

She sighed into the phone. "Thanks. The thing is, my boyfriend had just broken up with me and I was so sure it was him who was the blockhead, not me. So, I guess I was trying to prove I didn't need him — not that he was at the ranch to see — and could snag myself a man any time I wanted." She giggled again, this time the sound not quite so grating. Sadder, maybe. "That didn't work out the way I had planned."

"Uh..." Try as he might, James couldn't think of a useful thing to say. That she hadn't been an idiot? That he was sorry for her?

"Skylar and I got talking and, yeah, we're both sorry. That's not how our mamas raised us."

His, either. James was pretty sure Dad would be tempted to take Tori over his knee if she pulled one like that. Not that his sister ever would.

"Anyway, I tried to make a reservation for next year before we left, but your mom said there were no available cabins."

James stifled a grin. Mama bears protected their cubs. Always.

"Now I'm glad she said no, and I respect it. I really do. Your family seems cool, not like most I've met. Your parents seem to adore each other, even though your dad is crippled." Bailey's voice sounded wistful.

James knew a hurting soul and a nudge from God when he met one. "That's what true love is all about, you know. It's not just an attraction to physical looks or charm, but a deep, enduring bond no matter what happens in life."

She was silent a moment. "What happened to him?"

"Farm machine accident. His legs got caught in an

auger when the guy he was working with flicked the on switch by accident."

"That's terrible!"

It had been rough. More for Dad and Mom than the rest of them, but the reality of nearly losing their father had been traumatic on James and his sisters. The road to recovery had been long and painful... and never quite complete. "My parents have a strong faith, and that's what saw them through the darkest days. Knowing that if he died, he'd be in God's presence, and that if he lived, God would give him daily strength to face the pain and problems."

"I just can't even imagine how awful it must have been. I don't think most people would stick around."

"Most people I know would. I'm sure you've heard the wedding vows. They include words like for better, for worse, in sickness and in health, as long as we both shall live. If that's not sticking around, I don't know what is."

"You hang around different people than I do." This time, it wasn't his imagination. The attempt at light laughter was forced. "It seems everyone I know is divorced. Both my parents are on their third marriages."

"It doesn't have to be that way. I know plenty of people who aren't Christians but have stayed married, even through difficult times. I do believe having a shared faith goes a long way to providing a solid foundation for marital longevity, though."

"I've always thought of Christianity as something to mock, like people who need a crutch to get through life. No offense to your dad."

"There's far more to it. Yes, we do depend on God. You can call that a crutch if you like, but to me, it's more like having my priorities straight."

"Sounds weird. Like a total shift."

Whoever would have thought James would feel sorry for Bailey and ask the Lord to reveal Himself to her? Yet, now, he prayed for her. "I can send you a link to more information if you're interested."

Her voice perked up. "Would you?"

"Yeah, no problem. I can get your email address from the records, if that's okay."

"Sure. Thanks. And, James?"

"Yes?"

"I really did like it in Montana. It's so different from Chicago. The mountains are gorgeous, and the air is so refreshing. Everything is peaceful. Your chef at the ranch restaurant is outstanding. I've put a five-star review on Trip Advisor."

"Aw, thanks, Bailey. I'm glad you had a good time. It sounds like there might have been a reason for everything."

"That's a weird thought, isn't it? Thanks for being so gracious, James. I don't deserve it."

"It's okay." He could hardly believe he could say that and mean it. "Thanks for calling. I'll email you tomorrow."

Before the music could auto-resume, James tapped the pause icon and stared out at the darkening lake. Yes, it was gorgeous, refreshing, peaceful... everything Bailey had said. He could thank God he'd been born to a ranch family, that his parents loved each other, the Lord, their kids, and the land. Even without Lauren in his life, he was truly blessed.

He resumed play on the instrumentals as an engine started and a vehicle left the Flying Horseshoe. Sounded like a Wrangler. He'd been caught off guard more than once this week. The rumble of the Jeep owned by the folks in Cabin Four sounded just like Lauren's.

Chapter 20

James's voice replayed in Lauren's head all night long.

I can get your email address from the records, if that's okay ... Aw, thanks, Bailey. I'm glad you had a good time. It sounds like there might have been a reason for everything ... It's okay. Thanks for calling. I'll email you tomorrow.

I'm glad you had a good time. I'll email you tomorrow.

I'll email you tomorrow.

Bailey and James. The brazen blonde in Java Springs. Maybe Lauren had been right in the first place, that James had only looked uncomfortable because she'd caught him. It just didn't add up. He didn't talk to Bailey like a man in love, but they were clearly communicating. Phoning. Emailing. Lauren had just enough doubt that she'd paused on the sidewalk and listened before retreating.

She could be wrong, but she knew what she'd heard. James wasn't the kind of guy who'd email a girl without good reason. He didn't really text, either. He was so bad at communication.

That gave Lauren pause. Was he bad at telling her how he felt? His eyes certainly said things his words didn't. What of Bailey, then?

Lauren pounded her pillow. Why hadn't she marched up his steps and asked whom he was talking to? Why had she chickened out and aborted her mission? She'd been right there, hugging ninety-nine percent of her nerve. Now she had to do the whole thing over again, because she hadn't blurted out the apology she'd been rehearsing all the way to the ranch.

Her alarm buzzed, and she glared at it. Had she slept at all? If she had, she couldn't remember it. She'd looked at the clock at least once per hour. And now she had to go to work, be professional, and act like nothing had happened. She might be able to make an excuse to stop by the Flying Horseshoe today, but it was a bad idea. With Independence Day coming up, this was the busiest time at the guest ranch. She wouldn't be able to claim James's full attention for even five minutes.

She should've just gone for it last night, even with what she'd overheard.

Lauren was still beating herself up over it an hour later when she rolled into her parking spot behind the veterinary clinic, curls still damp and the wrapper from a protein bar still clutched in her hand. She grabbed her purse and to-go coffee cup, headed into the clinic, and greeted Milly at the front desk before heading down the corridor.

Wyatt Torrington's office door stood ajar. "Tomorrow night, then? I'll pick you up at five."

"I'm looking forward to it," Lauren's mom replied.

Wait a sec. Who? What? Lauren backed up a few steps and nudged the door open to see her colleague and her mom embrace each other. No stinkin' way. "What's going on here?"

Mom turned in Wyatt's arms and smiled at Lauren. "I was going to call you soon, promise."

All Lauren could manage was raising her eyebrows. Life was full of curve balls lately. This one came a close second to James. Both needed a good night's sleep to absorb, rest she hadn't received. She backed out of Wyatt's office, ready to scrub her eyes to remove the vision of what she'd seen.

"Wait, Lauren."

Even though she was an equal partner, she was conditioned to respect the man who'd been her father's best friend and associate, a man who'd known her since her birth. "Yes?"

"I know this comes as a shock to you, and I hope it isn't too awkward."

Oh, it was weird, all right. "A bit of a surprise, yes." Wyatt's wife had divorced him several years back, citing that he was married to his work. If anyone could understand a veterinarian's hours and life, it should be someone like Mom, who'd lived it.

Wyatt glanced down at Mom then back to Lauren. "I want you to know I have the greatest respect for your mother. We haven't been sneaking around. Tomorrow will be our first date. In fact..." He hesitated.

At least half the town didn't already know. Lauren crossed her arms over her chest. "I see." She didn't.

"You might remember my son, Luke."

She did. Luke had been several years ahead of her gang in school, a brilliant nerd. She nodded... whatever Luke had to do with this conversation.

"He's down for a few days over the Fourth, first time in a long time. Would you...?"

Mom leaned forward. "What Wyatt's trying to ask is if you would join us for dinner with Luke as your date?" She gave Lauren a pointed look.

Wyatt chuckled. "Yes, that's what I was getting to. I promised him a good time here, and I know you're the life of every party you attend."

At least she had someone fooled. "I, um..." She should just say no. Going out with Luke, even with their parents — weird — sent a signal to all of Saddle Springs, to James. Was that a signal she wanted sent?

Tori and Denae had urged her to date someone else to make James jealous. He'd never believe if she went out with Garret. He might believe with Luke, but she didn't want to make James jealous. She just wanted him to love her, which seemed too much to ask.

Lauren stared back at Mom and Wyatt. Her mouth was probably open. What was she supposed to say to this? It was only one date. Not even really a date — it didn't count if they were with their parents, did it?

Mom leaned out of Wyatt's arm and whispered, "Remember, you promised."

She'd promised if Mom started dating, she would, too. And, besides, it was only one evening, with a guy who lived in New York, of all places. This wasn't going to lead anywhere, and she could definitely explain it away to anyone who asked. "I, um, I guess that would be okay. Where are we going?"

Wyatt smiled and nodded, obviously relieved. "The Branding Iron, and then to the concert in the park."

In other words, where every single person in Saddle Springs would see them and speculate. Lovely.

Mom pursed her lips as her gaze slid the length of Lauren's body. "Dress up, darling. Luke's used to having a glamorous woman on his arm. That turquoise dress would be perfect."

For sitting on a blanket at the park? But Lauren nodded dumbly. She'd give her mom this one win. She'd promised, after all. That would be the end. After that, she'd find James and see if she could fix things. At the very least, she needed to apologize.

JAMES KEPT a close eye on Nelly as she plodded in circles in the corral, a beaming child on her broad back.

"My turn, Unca James!" wheedled Aiden from the corral rail.

"Not yet. Stay put."

"Good job, sweetie!" called the girl's mother as Tori led Coaldust past, with Matt and Luna right behind her. Today Matt would be leading the trail ride as all the guests who were participating had ridden a few times before. Good thing, as neither James nor Tori were willing to leave the main yard. They hadn't met their tiny niece yet, and the busiest weekend of the year wasn't enough to force them toward duty. The guests seemed to understand.

A yellow Honda turned off Creighton Road.

"Mommy!" yelled Aiden, turning to scramble down the rails. "Daddy!"

Tori thrust Coaldust's reins at Matt and vaulted the fence to catch Aiden before he ran into the car's path. She was quicker than James, who was still reaching to lift the little girl off Nelly's back. "Want to see a brand new teensy tiny baby?" Maybe that would mollify the child at the abrupt end to her riding lesson.

"We all do," the mother said with a grin, holding her hand out to her small daughter.

Across the yard, Mom and Dad came out onto the porch of the main house as the car pulled to a stop. Eli jogged around the car to get Meg's door, but not before Tori had opened the back door and released the baby's car seat.

"Oh, she's darling!" cooed Tori, fumbling with the five-point harness buckles.

Aiden pointed at the seat. "Aiden sistow." He nodded emphatically. "Baby."

"You got it, buddy. Let's have a look."

"I told you no one cared about me anymore," Meg said with a laugh.

James turned toward his sister. He'd probably been just as excited as Aiden was now when their parents had brought little Megan home from the hospital. He didn't remember, as he'd only been two. He remembered Tori, though. Remembered him and Meggie holding hands as they peered at the red-faced squalling infant. He hadn't been all that impressed, frankly. It had taken a few years for Tori to grow on him.

"Hey, Meg." He gave her a quick side hug. "Good job."

Meanwhile Tori had the baby out of the seat and in her arms, where she knelt to show Aiden. "She's perfect," she breathed.

James waited as long as he could handle it then tapped Tori's shoulder. "My turn."

"You?" She gave him an innocent look.

He raised his eyebrows and reached for the baby. Tori settled Sophia Grace into the crook of his arm as the baby stretched, arching her back, little fists flailing for a second. Then her eyes fixed on his, and James was a goner. "Hey, little princess," he whispered. "I'm your uncle James. Your protector."

The only thing that could be more perfect was if this was his child. His and Lauren's. The longing for Lauren had not diminished, no matter how many times James prayed. And this experience, holding his newborn niece in his arms? This made the hole in his life the most painful, the most poignant.

James was almost thirty years old. Life was passing him by, but no more. He'd make one last ditch effort to let Lauren know how much he loved her. He wouldn't stop until all the words had poured out, until he'd touched her, held her in his arms and, yes, kissed her. If she walked away for good, it would be because she didn't love him back. He'd make sure she knew exactly what she was turning down.

The thought of his dreams shut down forever clogged his throat and brought tears to his eyes. He clutched the precious bundle more tightly, and she whimpered.

"Sorry, princess," he whispered.

"Look, James is so overcome he's going to cry," teased Tori. "Don't get weepy all over the baby, big brother. Here, let me take her to Mom."

He shifted Sophia to Tori's arms and turned aside to blink away his emotions.

Eli gave him a lopsided grin. "A baby does that to a guy."

"Yeah. She's really something else. You take care of her, you hear me?"

"I think you're talking about Sophia, not Meg."

"Well, both of them, I guess." James shook his head then watched his sisters stroll up the steps to the ranch house together.

Eli scooped Aiden onto his shoulders, still focused on James. "So, what're you going to do?"

James grimaced. "I want what you've got, man. A wife. A monkey like this one." He chucked Aiden under the chin then twitched his head to indicate the group on the porch. "A princess like that one."

"I'm thankful," Eli said simply. "God has given me far more than I deserve."

"More than Meg deserves, too." How had the rebel of the family gotten so lucky? She mightn't have been married when Aiden was born, but there was no denying what a blessing the little boy was to his mommy and everyone around them.

"Yeah, God reminds me He doesn't look at us like that. None of it is about what we deserve. We haven't earned any of it. God looks at us and sees Jesus. Simple as that."

"Simple, but kinda profound."

Eli grinned. "I have my moments."

Chapter 21

Denae perched on the edge of Lauren's bed, holding Felix. "You look amazing, girlfriend. You're going all out here."

Was that a good thing or not? Lauren twirled in front of the mirror, the chiffon over-skirt swishing against her knees.

"If you're trying to make James notice, I believe you'll succeed. Even I'm not completely sure what you're up to, and I'm in on it. I think." Denae squeezed the cat until he squirmed and grumbled.

"I'm not doing this to make James jealous. I'm doing it because I made a deal with my mom that I thought would never happen. She hasn't dated since my dad died fifteen years ago, so I thought I was safe."

"Ooh, that's one of my favorite things to find in a romance novel. An ill-advised pact."

Lauren glared at her friend. "Stuff it. I'm not in the mood. Tonight is not going to be romantic. Not even a tiny bit. I'm enduring it because I gave my word to my mom."

"I'm just saying..."

"Don't."

"All right then. Tell me all about it when you get home, okay?"

"Aren't you coming to the festivities in the park? It's the Fourth."

Denae shrugged. "I have a deadline, and no one to go with."

"You can meet me there."

"Right. You're on a hot date with Mr. Manhattan, and you want a third wheel? I'm thinking not."

"Please don't sit home alone while the town is celebrating. That's just un-American."

"Oh, there'll be fireworks in the story I'm editing." Denae grinned, waggling her eyebrows. "I'll have a great time by proxy."

The doorbell rang, and Lauren whirled back to the mirror. She didn't wear a lot of makeup — had she even put it on right? She scrunched her curls. They were as good as they were going to get. Now, where were her shoes? Why wasn't she ready before Luke got here?

She grabbed the straps of her sandals and jogged to the front of the duplex, took two seconds to compose herself, and opened the door.

Gone was the tall, gangly, slightly awkward teen she remembered. Today's Luke Torrington was tanned, muscular, and glasses-free. He smiled at her — a gorgeous smile — and held out a bouquet of bright, happy gerbera daisies. "Lauren? Good to see you again. It's been a while."

"Hi, Luke. Come on in for a minute, and I'll put these in water. They're exquisite." She'd read that line in a few novels, but never imagined she'd be the one saying them. She also had never thought she'd be thankful for the kind of mother who thought every woman should own a few pieces of crystal, but at least there was a cut-glass vase in her cabinet.

Lauren pulled out the vase, filled it with water, and arranged the blooms with shaking fingers. At least the act gave her something to focus on, something that didn't include her stammering and staring at the unlikely man who leaned casually against her kitchen doorjamb, hands in the pockets of gray slacks. When was the last time she'd seen a guy who wasn't in jeans?

Cheri and Kade's wedding.

She pushed the thought of James in a tailored black suit out of her mind. Tomorrow she'd be free of her obligations and could focus on him, on trying to build a relationship on a solid foundation, if one could be had. Today, she needed to be nice to Luke. Thankfully, it didn't look like it would be much of a hardship.

Lauren centered the bouquet on her table and smiled at Luke. "Thank you. I wasn't expecting flowers."

He tilted his head and smiled back before rolling back a white sleeve and glancing at his gold watch. "Ready? I told Dad we'd meet them at The Branding Iron."

She slipped the sandals on her feet. "Ready."

He offered his elbow, and she took it, thankful for the

assistance as she navigated with unfamiliar heels. The sight of a sleek red convertible at the curb nearly did her in. Obviously, the Luke Torrington who'd left Saddle Springs a nerdy teen had met with some success in the intervening years. Only question was, why hadn't some girl snatched him up already?

Luke helped her into the car, rounded it, and got in. As he pulled away from the curb, he asked, "Is it just me, or is the thought of our parents dating kind of awkward?"

She chuckled. "My dad died when I was fifteen. To the best of my knowledge, this is the first time my mom's gone out since."

"Your father was one of the good ones."

Of course, he'd known Dad. Lauren had forgotten their shared background for a few minutes. "I take it you didn't follow in your father's footsteps."

Luke shook his head. "No, I went into investment banking. A lot different than being in smelly barns at any time of day or night, regardless of the weather."

"I love it," she said softly. "I never wanted to do anything else."

"Good for you." Luke shot her a look. "I know my father appreciates having you for his partner. Thanks for that — it makes up for how much I've disappointed him."

Lauren turned and looked at him. "I can't imagine he's disappointed in you."

He parked the convertible in front of The Branding Iron. "He doesn't understand my choices. Thinks my mother had a bad influence on me." Luke offered a wry grin. "Did your mom ever hassle you for following in your dad's footsteps?"

Lauren thought back, slowly shaking her head. "No. My mom has a lot of opinions — brace yourself for them — but, really, all she wanted for me was to follow God's will for my life."

Luke's eyebrows rose. "It's been a while since I heard that term. Sounds a bit like a cop-out. Sorry if that offends you."

"No, I understand that it sounds weird. The thing is... you went to church when you lived here, didn't you?" Sounded like that no longer held true.

He grimaced. "Fourth row on the far right, every Sunday."

"Right. It's taken me a long time to think deeply on God's plan and how it relates to my own will. Like, what happens if I willfully disobey what I know God wants me to do? Or what if I didn't ask and go the wrong way? Can I ever get back in His good graces?"

Any hint of a smile had long since fled Luke's face. "Too deep for me."

"Important questions."

"No, what's important is making the world a better place than you found it. Honesty, compassion, and loyalty."

"Those are good things, for sure." Lauren chose her words carefully, becoming more sure of them with every word uttered. "But what God really wants of us is a relationship with Him. Everything else is secondary."

Luke shook his head and pointed toward the restaurant. "I suggest we table this discussion before our parents decide we've stood them up. Ready?"

At her nod, he came around the car, opened the door, then ushered her into The Branding Iron.

JAMES SETTLED on a quilt between Kade and Tori, listening to Cheri and Carmen chat while their little daughters played nearby. He couldn't remember a time when getting the gang together didn't include Lauren. He hadn't dared phone her to make sure she was coming, hoping against hope that tradition would win out.

Tori's phone chimed with an incoming text as he took a quick scan around the fairgrounds while pretending not to be hunting for Lauren. His gaze froze on a couple entering the gate in the distance. Lauren. It had to be, with her short dark curls and that gorgeous turquoise dress he'd never been able to get out of his mind, but with whom? How could she be laughing up at a tall stranger who looked like a city businessman compared to any cowboy in Saddle Springs?

"Uh oh," whispered Tori, nudging him.

"Who is that?" he asked under his breath, careful not to move his mouth. If only he could stop staring.

"Denae just texted. She was there when he picked Lauren up. That's Luke Torrington, back for the weekend visiting his dad. Look, there's Lauren's mom and Doc behind them."

Did that make it better or worse? Lauren turned to

say something to her mother. Luke's hand rested on the small of her back.

Red blood pulsed through James's vision.

"Denae's drooling," whispered Tori. "She says Luke's the hunkiest hunk she ever did see."

"Looks like he's taken," growled James.

Tori pressed against his arm. "Don't believe everything you see."

"Right." Because that made a ton of sense. Lauren had been pushing James away for a year or two. Was it because she'd been in a long-distance relationship with Luke Torrington all this time? He didn't want to think that of her, but it only made sense. She was a stunning, vibrant woman. She was plenty good enough to catch the eye of a Manhattan millionaire. James had heard rumors of the small-town boy making it big.

"She's not in love with Luke."

James leaned away from his sister, finally managing to look toward the bandstand instead of the gate. "You can't know that."

"I *do* know."

"I think... whatever we thought we knew, wasn't all the truth." The realization bashed him like a sledgehammer. He'd thought he knew Lauren. Obviously, he hadn't. At all. If she had her sights set on a guy like Luke, there was no hope for James. He was a cowboy, for heaven's sake. He hadn't made a fortune in finance or in anything else. He all but lived with his parents and hadn't ventured out of western Montana in years. Whatever else was true, he wasn't in Luke Torrington's league. If Lauren wasn't on the guy's arm, James would totally be fine with his own choices. But glitz had won the girl. *James's* girl.

The furious jealousy plummeted into depressing, mind-numbing reality. The thought of sitting here with his friends listening to some stupid bluegrass band and pretending to celebrate his nation's birthday repelled him.

He rose to his feet. "I'm sorry. I'm going back home."

His friends stared up at him, eyes wide, mouths open. Maybe they said something. He didn't know. Couldn't hear over the pounding in his skull.

Tori hopped up. "I'm coming, too."

"No need."

"What's going on?" asked Cheri.

James strode away, thankful for other exits from the fairgrounds, even though it meant going the long way around to get to his truck. Didn't matter. All that mattered was getting out of here, saddling Jigsaw, and going for a run. Yeah, it would be dark soon. Who cared? The mare knew her way, and the moon would rise eventually.

He had some thinking to do. Maybe some yelling at God. Maybe even a few tears.

After seeing James stride out of the fairgrounds at the farthest gate from the parking area, Tori jogging behind him, Lauren knew she'd blown it, but what was she supposed to do now? Desert Luke, run after James, and make a scene? She might've done just that if her mother hadn't spoken right then, pulling her attention. When she next looked, James and Tori had disappeared.

Luke guided her to a quilt his dad had spread for the four of them, thankfully a long distance from where Carmen and Cheri watched with curious expressions. Kade's arms were crossed below a scowling face. The others stared.

Trying to swallow the lump in her throat, Lauren sat angled away from them. She'd make it up to them — everyone — later. At least, if they let her. Most important was James. Only a few hours before, she'd spouted talk of God's will at Luke. Now she had to wonder if she'd blindly obeyed her mother when her heart said otherwise. Had she asked the Lord for guidance? Her heart sank. Not really.

She'd blown it. Again. Maybe this time for good.

The band struck up. Guitars, fiddles, banjos. Guys with long hair and tight jeans who didn't have half the voice James did. Couldn't play as well.

Lauren longed for the evening to be over. She felt trapped. Maybe James had, too. Maybe that's why he escaped. She could take a break at intermission and visit her friends, but she wasn't ready for all the accusations they'd fling her way, all the explanations they'd refuse to hear. She could excuse herself to the restroom and keep walking, but not in these heels. Not the mile or two back to the condo. Although maybe Denae would come get her if she asked.

Instead, she smiled at something Luke said and tried

not to notice Wyatt's arm braced behind her mother as they laughed together.

Survival. That was tonight's only goal. Tomorrow things would look better. They had to.

These weren't the fireworks James had planned to view tonight. Pain shot through him and hammered his head as he lay on his back staring up into the darkness. What kind of an idiot galloped his horse at night, when neither could see where they were going?

He'd taken Jigsaw out on Creighton Road. The smooth blacktop should have been safe enough. Definitely a better choice than a mountain trail with roots and rocks. All had been well until... what had spooked the mare?

It hurt to think, but a vague memory of a full spread of owl wings whooshing right over his head presented itself. Jigsaw had reared in panic. James had been too shocked, too distracted to keep his seat.

He hurt everywhere.

Where was his horse? He rolled over and pushed himself to sitting. His head swam, and the fireworks crescendoed. "Jigsaw?"

Silence and darkness. Great. How was he going to get home? He flexed one arm slowly, then the other. Rotated his shoulders. So far, so good. Gingerly, he stretched his left leg and caught his breath. Wow, that ankle hurt. He traced the joint with his hands. It seemed at the correct angle. The right leg was okay.

Fine. He needed to get upright and figure out where he was. He'd turned around a few miles up the road. Was he anywhere near the new building site or Meg and Eli's? If so, he might have coverage. He patted his shirt pocket, thankful he kept it snapped over his phone.

One bar. Who to call? Tori would scold him like a mother hen. His brother-in-law was likely the closest and least judgmental. James tapped Eli's number.

Chapter 22

Lauren hurried into the clinic the next morning, juggling her purse and her coffee. Finally, the horrible holiday weekend was over, and life would get back to normal, or at least as close as possible with her partner dating her mother. She gave her head a quick shake, trying to dislodge last night's images. A full round of calls would keep her mind off James until evening, and then she'd figure out what to do and how to do it.

If he were talking to her at all.

No. She pushed the thought out of her mind as the phone rang and Milly answered it.

"Saddle Springs Veterinary. Milly speaking." The receptionist mouthed *good morning* at Lauren. "Oh, no! I'm sorry to hear that. I can send one of the vets out right away. I believe Doctor Yanovich is most familiar with Jigsaw."

Jigsaw? James's horse? Lauren set the coffee cup down

on the divider with a thud. No matter how tightly she tuned in, she couldn't make out the caller's voice. Her mind buzzed as Milly finished up the call and set the receiver down.

"That was Amanda Carmichael out at the Flying Horseshoe. I didn't catch exactly what happened, but Jigsaw got out somehow and came back this morning limping. Do you mind checking her out?"

"I'm on my way." Her coveralls and medical bag lived in the back of the Wrangler. All that was needed was her. She grabbed her coffee and jogged out to the Jeep.

The Flying Horseshoe yard was quiet for the day after a major holiday. Maybe everyone was out on a trail ride or something. A quick scan didn't reveal James or Tori, so she headed to the stable.

James's mom stepped out of the office at Lauren's approach. "Over here. Poor beauty."

"What happened?" Lauren set down her bag and took a good look at Jigsaw. The horse seemed reluctant to put weight on her front left leg, and her head drooped. Lauren glanced at James's mom.

Amanda shook her head. "I don't know how much to tell you. James went out for a ride last night and took a tumble. He managed to get a hold of Eli, who brought him home, but they couldn't find the mare. Jigsaw showed up about an hour ago a little worse for a night in the wild."

Lauren's mouth opened and snapped shut. She'd wager a bet James hadn't pitched off Jigsaw's back in all the years since the mare was green broke. How had that possibly happened? The vision of his square back retreating last night settled in her memory. Was she responsible? And if that had been his reaction to seeing her with Luke, why did the thought make her heart despair and exult at the same time?

No matter. She was on the clock, and her first duty was to Jigsaw. She slid back the stall door and approached the mare, crooning softly.

***

Call him a glutton for punishment, but James couldn't resist making his slow way to the stable once he'd seen Lauren's Wrangler pull into the yard. He didn't even try to tell himself it was only concern for Jigsaw, although that was definitely a factor. No, he needed to see Lauren. Needed to see if she was happy, even if it killed him. Had he taken too long?

He winced, not just from the pain in his ankle. Of *course*, he'd taken too long. Fourteen years was at least five or ten too many. He was some kind of idiot.

James paused before entering the stable and turned his eyes skyward. "God? I could use a hand here. Your will be done." It might've been a short prayer, but he meant it all the same.

Voices from the back corral lured him through the building and into the summer sunshine where Mom watched as Lauren led Jigsaw in a large circle, focused on the mare's steps. He came up beside his mother.

"Want me to stay?" Mom asked softly.

Did he? No. It was time to man up and lay it all out to the woman he loved. If she convinced him she loved Luke Torrington instead, his mom didn't need to bear witness. Likewise, if James finally — *finally* — had the opportunity to kiss Lauren with fourteen years' worth of pent-up emotion. He shook his head.

Mom squeezed his arm and slipped away, leaving James leaning on the rail, keeping the weight off his wrapped ankle. Watching Lauren put his horse through its paces, stroking the sore leg, pursing her lips. Then she looked over and realization dawned on her face. Awareness that Mom had stepped away, leaving James on guard.

"How is she?" James's voice sounded rusty to his own ears, like he hadn't used his vocal chords in a month, but he had. He'd done a lot of yelling in the dark last night.

"Her muscles are strained, but I think she'll be okay with some rest. We'll watch for inflammation and do what we can to keep her leg cool."

He liked the sound of that 'we.'

Lauren stepped closer, the mare at her heels. She slipped a piece of apple to Jigsaw, who eagerly filched it. Then she was standing in front of him, a four-rail, chest-high fence between them.

He should have gone inside the corral while she wasn't looking. That barrier might as well be a mountain with his sore ankle.

She was so close he could smell vanilla shampoo over the aroma of horse. "Lauren."

"What happened?"

It took him a second to realize she meant Jigsaw. What had Mom told her? It didn't much matter. This was his moment. "The short version or the long one?"

Her gaze flicked to his face then down at the reins in her hands. "Whichever you want."

"I love you, Lauren."

The words hung in the air. One second. Two seconds. Three. Maybe she wasn't ready to hear it.

"You do?" Her voice squeaked, just a little.

"I've loved you for half my life. I told myself I was being a good guy, allowing you to find your own way to happiness, whether that was with me or someone else, but I know now it was the chicken's way out. How could you know if I never told you?"

She sucked in her bottom lip.

The sight killed him. "Last night I saw you with Luke. That's when I knew I was too late. I did something stupid. Took Jigsaw out on the road at a full canter. An owl swooped us, she reared, and I hit the blacktop. She bolted."

Lauren fingered the reins.

Why didn't she say anything? Maybe he really was too late. An enormous lump stuck in his throat, and he took a step back. "I just wanted you to know." Another step back.

Less talking. More kissing. Had that been Meg's advice or Tori's? Maybe both of them. But that was before Luke Torrington. It also didn't account for a stupid corral fence. Another step back.

She stood there, frozen, staring at the ground. Like a statue.

Had he really said everything he needed to say? Words, yeah. But not emotions. He was a guy. He was bad at feelings. But if getting the emotions out — or not — was what stood between him and the woman he loved, then he needed to get over it.

Now.

He'd promised himself it would be all on the line. He'd promised God.

The gate was too far around. James put one foot on the second rail and hoisted himself up. Then over. Instead of hopping off the top like he normally would, he lowered himself a bit more carefully. That ankle stung like crazy.

He tugged the reins from Lauren's passive hands and looped them over the nearest post then turned back toward her. "Lauren. Did you hear me? I love you." And then he rested his hands on her waist and gave a little tug.

She stumbled forward, and her gaze caught on his, her eyes wide.

At least now she was looking up. He'd never before considered how hard it might be to kiss a woman who stared at the ground. Giving her just enough time to duck away if she wanted to, he lowered his head until his mouth covered hers.

Half a lifetime of longing surged within him, but he held back until her lips became pliant under his. At her slightest response, he pulled her closer, wrapping his arms around her, holding her securely.

Lauren's lips parted, and she kissed him back. Not like a woman who was in love with some other guy, some city slicker, but like a woman who wanted to be right here, right now. With James.

James loved her.

The words ricocheted around in Lauren's mind like bolts of lightning. He loved her. He held her close, hands splayed over her back, his lips daring her not to believe the words they'd spoken.

He loved her. She could taste it on his persuasive mouth. Smell it on his minty-fresh breath. Feel it in the way their bodies melded as his hands smoothed her coveralls and gathered her ever tighter.

She couldn't say how long they stood there, kissing like they had a decade to make up for. Then Jigsaw whuffled over Lauren's shoulder, tickling her ear with warm, moist breath. Lauren giggled against James's mouth and felt his lips curve upward.

She opened her eyes to see his grin. "Jigsaw approves. Not that I much care."

The mare nickered, and James reached over and nudged her head away. Then his forehead rested on Lauren's, and he looked deeply into her eyes. "Please tell me you love me."

Was this real? Or was she going to wake up with a tear-soaked pillow and a headache the size of Montana?

Those blue eyes, so intense beneath his cowboy hat, looked clear into her soul. "Lauren?"

If this were a dream, she could say whatever she wanted, and he'd never be the wiser. Right? "I love you, James Carmichael."

Relief eased over his features. "You had me worried there for a minute." His mouth curved upward amid his neatly trimmed beard.

"I didn't mean to." She touched a finger gently to his lips. "I can't believe this is real. That you're real."

"Believe it." He kissed her, shorter this time, but no less persuasively.

Her legs nearly buckled beneath her. She'd laughed when Denae talked about heroines who swooned. Chalk one up for first-hand knowledge. Lauren fisted his denim shirt. Was it to keep him close and kissable, or was it to keep upright? She wasn't sure, but *yes* to more kissing.

"So, how's Jig... Oh, never mind." Tori's voice.

Lauren tried to pull away — okay, she didn't try that hard — but James took his time releasing her lips. His eyes twinkled at Lauren before turning to take in his sister. "Did you want something? Kind of busy here."

"Well, let me be the first to congratulate you both on coming to your senses. I've never seen anyone so dense before, but you two made me wonder if there was any hope for the human race. Or at least the part of the human race with the surname Carmichael."

Lauren's cheeks warmed, and she turned her face away from Tori.

James chuckled and pressed her head against his

chest, tangling his fingers in her short curls. "Just because we don't jump at your command doesn't mean there's no hope, sis. How about you take Jigsaw back to her stall and make yourself scarce?"

Tori laughed. "I'll take her, though she seems inordinately interested in what you two are doing. But I'll warn you, Matt and the trail riders will be back any minute, so I'm not sure you really want to keep smooching in a busy, stinky corral. Sorry, Jigsaw. It's true."

"Good point." James looped his arm around Lauren's shoulder and took a step toward the gate before he grimaced.

She looked up at him. "You okay?"

"Not exactly. Let's just say Creighton Road isn't a soft place to land when you and your horse part ways unexpectedly."

"Aw, you poor baby." Tori's voice took on a slightly sarcastic air. "Did anyone ever tell you riding full tilt at night was a bad idea, or did you just figure that out for yourself? Lauren, take this poor cowboy out of here. Make him put his feet up or something. He's off duty today."

Realization and responsibility swept over Lauren. "Oh! I'm not."

James's fingers massaged her shoulder as he limped out of the corral with her at his side. "Busy day at the clinic?"

"There's always plenty going on." Skipping out would be fun. Wyatt would be okay... right? No, Lauren was a grownup. A partner in the business. She tugged James toward the Wrangler in the parking lot. "I should get back to work."

He gathered her close and kissed her again. "Come back as soon as you're off?"

"I'll bring pizza," she promised.

"Deal." He opened the Jeep door for her. "Extra pepperoni—"

"And add jalapeños." She knew the drill. She knew this man… better than she ever had before.

Lauren glanced out the side window as she turned onto the road toward Saddle Springs. James stood in the middle of the gravel parking lot watching her. He grinned and lifted his hand as she drove around the next bend.

She squealed and drummed her hands on the steering wheel as soon as he was out of sight. James loved her. She loved him. Finally, *finally*, the future looked bright.

Chapter 23

"Ready to get wet?" Kade held Cheri over the end of the dock jutting into the small lake in the moonlight. She squealed and clutched his neck.

"Water's great!" called Denae, although James noticed she'd grabbed a terry cover-up since her last swim.

He and Eli had built the new dock in the cove between their two houses — a place to launch early morning paddles and fishing expeditions, a place to swim. Maybe they'd build a raft like the one across by the resort someday, but James hadn't had time to get overly nostalgic about old times in the two weeks since he and Lauren had first kissed. This dock had already been half-built. He'd just needed incentive to finish it off, and he'd had that in spades.

Lauren. She leaned back against his chest right now, nestled between his drawn-up knees. James's heart hadn't stopped soaring since the fifth of July, the day after he'd thought his hopes dissolved forever. He nuzzled her short, curly hair then found her neck, marveling that the Lord had finally nudged them together.

Kade leaped off the dock, still holding a kicking Cheri. They bobbed up seconds later, flicking wet hair off their faces. Cheri dove at Kade, grabbed his head, and dunked him again. Garret dove in, followed by Carmen. Much splashing ensued.

"James?" Lauren whispered against his cheek.

His arms clenched around her. "Hmm?"

"Thank you for loving me."

"My pleasure." He trailed kisses down her neck. "Want to swim? Promise I won't throw you in."

She shivered. "I'm done, I think. Just enjoying sitting here. With you."

"Like old times, only better." Much better, because he'd never had the pleasure of Lauren relaxing against him any other time their group had gotten together. A few friends from their teen years had left Saddle Springs, and several new ones had joined them. They were older now, responsible adults. Behind them on the hillside, James's new house had begun to take shape. The house where, if all went well, he and Lauren would live, love, and raise a family.

In the water, Cheri wrapped her arms around Kade as they kissed. Their relationship had turned out different than anyone expected back in high school, but look at them now, passionately in love and building a home — made of timber and made of trust — for their family. Tonight, they'd hired a teen babysitter for their two and Carmen's daughter, who was enjoying a sleepover.

"Much better than old times," murmured Lauren. "Need me to help with the cake or anything?"

James angled a glance at the moon. Almost time. "I've got it, birthday girl. It will only take a few minutes to set out."

"It's your birthday, too."

And one he'd never forget. "Thirty. Crazy, huh?" he said lightly.

Kade hoisted himself onto the dock, gave Cheri a hand up, then wrapped her in a huge towel. Everyone else clambered onto the deck as well. Laughing. Talking. Tossing towels.

"Excuse me a minute," James whispered to Lauren as he relinquished his hold and rose to his feet. "Need to toss a few logs on the fire. Get ready for phase three."

She grinned up at him, and that was nearly enough for him to gather her in and kiss her again. But... not now. In a minute. Phase one had been hot dogs and potato salad by the fire. Phase two had been playing and swimming. Phase three... James's gut tightened. More than cupcakes were at stake here, but he'd start with those. The guest ranch chef, Ollie, had arranged the tiered platter and packed freshly-churned ice cream in its own ice-filled cooler.

James poked at the fire and set a few more pieces of split wood on it. Flames licked at the logs then flared, crackling. He looked up at the sky, where sparks joined the stars. "Thank you, Lord. So many blessings."

"Amen," whispered Lauren, her arm sliding around his waist.

James gathered her close. "I thought I told you to stay put."

"I thought you knew I wasn't very obedient."

He laughed and kissed her. "You're right. I did know that. Call everyone together, and we'll have dessert?"

She looked at him quizzically then nodded, heading back to the dock.

James lifted the tiered dessert platter onto the folding table. He'd set up a gazebo earlier, lined with solar lights that had gathered sunshine all day and now offered a gentle glow to the buckets of ice where sparkling cider chilled beside wine goblets. The crowning touch on the cupcake on the top tier gleamed slightly in the soft lighting. James closed his eyes for a second, another brief prayer lifting. *Please, Lord.*

"Happy birthday to you!" Kade and Garret sang in harmony. Everyone joined in. "Happy birthday to you! Happy birthday James and Lauren; happy birthday to you!"

James held his arm out toward Lauren, and she stepped into it. She looked up at him, a contented smile on her lips — a look he couldn't resist. He bent and kissed her.

Sawyer whistled. Everyone laughed.

The moment of truth.

James turned Lauren toward the tiers of cupcakes and lifted the top one. "Happy birthday, my love." He held it out toward her.

She glanced at him then back at the cupcake as she reached for it.

He knew the exact second her eyes caught the glint of the diamond ring encircling the chocolate cowboy hat on top of the creamy frosting. He dropped to one knee, still holding it toward her.

Lauren snatched both her hands back and covered her face, eyes wide and bright in the low light.

"Lauren, I've loved you forever." James's voice caught, but he powered through. "Will you marry me?"

She danced a little jig right there on the spot, her hands still covering her mouth. "Oh, James..."

"Told you tonight was the night." Kade's voice sounded smug.

The rock James knelt on wasn't particularly soft, nor was his ankle completely healed. "Lauren?"

She leaned over him, caressing his face between both her hands. He closed his eyes, enjoying the gentle, loving touch. "Yes," she whispered, her lips brushing over his.

"High-five on it!" yelled Sawyer.

James pulled to his feet, plucked the ring off the top of the cupcake, and slid it on Lauren's finger. Her look of wonder and delight was all he'd hoped for.

"High-five. High-five. High-five," their friends chanted.

James held up both hands. With one final look at her gleaming left hand, Lauren slapped both her hands into his.

Cat-calls, whistles, and clapping crescendoed and faded away as he stepped closer, their hands still clasped as he lowered them. "I love you, Lauren." He pressed his lips to hers, aware of their audience. "Now, will you stop trying to foist me off on someone else?"

She smiled against his lips. "I'm fine with that. I believe you've found your perfect match." She whirled in his arms and faced their gathered friends. "But I'm not done with all of you yet. Some of you seem to need a bit of help."

Kade and Cheri smiled at each other. Tori groaned. Denae shook her finger. "Oh, no, you don't. I know all about how romance works, and interference from friends is no help."

"Oh, you know all about it, do you? With all your vast experience?" Tori challenged, grinning around at the group then back at Denae. "Seems to me there's more to love than book-learnin'. And don't mind me, folks, I'm the youngster of the bunch. I can wait my turn."

At everyone's laughter, James rested his hands on Lauren's hips and turned her toward him. "Happy?"

She set her hands on his shoulders, her gaze lingering on the ring before lifting to meet his. "So happy. I can't wait to be your bride. Did you have a date in mind?"

He shook his head. "Brent from Timber Framing Plus says the house should be move-in-ready by Christmas, but we don't have to use that as a gauge. I'm not sure I want to wait that long."

Lauren reached up and gave him a quick kiss. "Christmas sounds wonderful. A lot goes into planning a wedding. The time will go by quicker than you'd ever guess."

"I thought you might say that." James grinned ruefully. "And I think you're right. Oh, hey, you can take over making decisions about the house."

"I hope that's not why you asked me to marry you." Her eyebrows rose into her curly hair.

"Not a chance, but it will be a nice side benefit. This is what I'm really looking for." James slid his hands around her back and covered her mouth with his. Her eager lips met his, and he deepened the kiss. He kissed her thoroughly. "All I want is you."

ACKNOWLEDGMENTS

If you've read previous stories of mine, you'll know that cowboy romance is a minor variation on my usual themes of farm-and-garden such as in my flagship Farm Fresh Romance series. The Montana Ranches overlap slightly with both the Garden Grown Romances (part of the multi-author Arcadia Valley Romance series) where Cheri (Mackenzie) Delgado played a small role, and with the Urban Farm Fresh Romance series, where Denae Archibald appears as a friend to Sadie Guthrie in *Raindrops on Radishes*.

Thanks to Elizabeth Maddrey for being a sounding board and an encouraging first reader as well as a terrific author whose stories I enjoy reading!

I also appreciate my beta readers: Paula, Amy, Joelle, Debbie, and Karen. Thanks for loving this new direction, encouraging me, and catching my errors... although I'm sure I managed to leave a few in, even after my fabulous editor, Nicole, had her input. Thanks for sticking with me through all these years and stories, Nicole.

I'm also grateful for the Christian Indie Authors Facebook group and my sister bloggers at Inspy Romance. These folks make a difference in my life every single day. I'm thrilled to walk beside them as we tell stories for Jesus!

Thank you to my Facebook friends, followers, street team, and reader group members for prayers, encouragement, and great fellowship. If you'd like to join other readers who love my stories, please find us at https://valeriecomer.com/FBreaders.

Thanks to my husband, Jim, whose love for me never fails and who encourages me in every endeavor. Thanks to my kids, their spouses, and my wonderful grandgirls for cheering me on. To them, having an author for a mom/grandma is "normal." Imagine that!

All my love and gratitude goes to Jesus, the One who is my vision, the High King of Heaven, the lord of my heart. Thank you. A thousand times, thank you.

Enjoy this Book?

Please leave a review at any online retailer or reader site. Letting other readers know what you think about *The Cowboy's Mixed-Up Matchmaker: a Montana Ranches Christian Romance* helps them make a decision and means a lot to me. Thank you!

Keep reading for the first chapter of *The Cowboy's Romantic Dreamer,* the third book in the Saddle Springs Romance series.

Montana Ranches
Christian Romance Series

THE COWBOY'S
Romantic Dreamer

SADDLE SPRINGS ROMANCE - BOOK 3

USA Today Bestselling Author
VALERIE COMER

Chapter 1

Trevor Delgado liked all these people just fine, but when those two women started looking at each other that way, it made a guy nervous. They were creating a talent show. That should definitely let him off the hook, since he had no talents.

He was still nervous, even though he was poised to shake his head. *Ready, set, no.*

Lauren Carmichael and Denae Archibald weren't up on the meaning of *no*. They just figured a guy probably didn't understand enough to say *yes*. Any objections could be overcome.

They were wrong, but he'd hold out.

Denae turned to Cheri. "Would you be interested in donating a painting?"

Trevor's sister-in-law, Cheri, rubbed her hands across her round belly. "Probably. So long as this little one is patient about his or her arrival."

"The event isn't until the end of May, so you've got

lots of time." Lauren made a note on her tablet. "The baby's due in, what, ten weeks?"

"About that. May third."

Trevor tried to ignore his brother's arm slipping around Cheri's shoulder and tugging her close. Refused to notice the smile they shared. He was happy for Kade. Really, he was. The guy was such a sap it was hard not to cheer him on. He'd been in love with Cheri since they were teens, and they'd reunited a year ago. This baby would make three kids, rounding out his and hers with — finally — theirs. It had been a convoluted path to happily-ever-after.

He wasn't used to thinking in terms of that phrase, but Denae Archibald's re-entry into their group had expanded his vocabulary. Always more than willing to explain the ins and outs of character arcs and plot points from the romance novels she edited to anyone who would listen. Anyone who knew so much about romance ought to be happily married herself by now, but Denae was still on the manhunt.

Reason enough for Trevor to keep a low profile, not that she had designs on him. Like, who would? Of the three Delgado brothers, he was the eldest, the loner, the one too absorbed in riding the western Montana ranges to have a social life. He'd had a chance or two at relationships a few years back, blown it, and was going to stay a bachelor until he died.

Denae beamed at Cheri, her whole face lit by that megawatt smile, as though her friend's pregnancy was her personal joy in life. Course, she was probably the happiest person Trevor knew, which about drove him crazy. Her natural beauty did, too. She was tall and model-thin, with gorgeous black hair that cropped across her forehead in thick bangs just above her dark, sparkly eyes.

Not that Trevor noticed her sparkle. It was simply that she was different from all the girls he'd grown up with, an unknown entity. One he clearly needed to keep an eye on lest she rope him into something he'd later regret.

"We have you and Garret down for music."

Trevor's head jerked before he could control it. Before he saw Denae looking pointedly at James. Whew.

The other guys exchanged a glance and a shrug. "Sure."

"A solo, Kade?"

Kade furrowed his brow. "I don't know. I haven't done any public singing in a long time."

Here it came. Trevor planted his feet deeper into the plush area rug in front of the leather sofa, trying to keep his knee from jiggling. What should he do with his hands? Why wasn't he holding a mug to give them something to do?

"Maybe with Trev." Lauren's voice. "Haven't heard you two sing together in years."

"No." There. He'd gotten the word out. Now he simply had to stick to it against a stampede of yearling calves.

Denae's long black hair swung as she turned to face him. "You sing?"

"No."

"You used to," countered Lauren.

"Not anymore."

Denae frowned. "How can you just stop?"

"He hit puberty in front of the congregation on a Sunday morning." Kade chuckled. "We were singing a duet — what was it, Trev, Rock of Ages? — and his voice went all over the place. Up, squeak, down, squeak. It was hilarious."

"It wasn't funny," Trevor ground out. "Not even a little bit."

"Oh, man, it was, too. You need to learn to laugh at yourself."

Not happening. He raised his eyebrows and looked between Denae and Lauren. "To make a long story short, I'm not participating in your talent show. I also don't build stuff—" he made a tumbling motion "—to donate to the auction. I'll come. I'll bid on things. I'll heckle the participants, especially if one of them is my kid brother. But I'm not performing."

"Well, thanks." Kade laughed. "Not sure I can handle being up front without my big bro." He turned to Denae. "I'll think about it and see if I come up with anything. How secular an event is this? I mean, would it be okay to do a Christian song?"

"I don't see why not. It's family-friendly, so there are strictures against foul language and the like, but no one on the council said anything about spiritual content."

Across the room, Garret picked at a piece of fluff from the area rug where he sat crosslegged. "How come you're on the arts council anyway, Denae? I didn't know you were an artist."

Trevor didn't know that, either. Plus, he rather liked someone else being in the hot seat for a moment. It sure beat being picked on for a cracking adolescent voice. Having a chance to watch Denae without anyone noticing was a great benefit.

His hands stilled on his thighs.

Really? No way. She was just an unknown entity. Nothing more. There might be plenty of room in his house, but there wasn't room in his heart or life for a woman. They were too unpredictable.

Look at Cheri. She'd run off a week before her wedding to Kade, leaving his brother heartbroken. Yeah, they'd eventually reunited, but not after a lot of pain. Watching his brother's despair had nearly killed Trevor.

Look at Lauren. She said she'd loved James since they were teens, but wasn't pushing him off on other women for years a strange way to show it? Yeah, okay, they'd finally admitted their mutual adoration and been married last Christmas, but was the decade of agony worth it?

Trevor didn't do pain. He didn't do does-she-love-me-or-not games. He'd dabbled in that one once, gotten burned, and learned his lesson. He wasn't stupid enough to blindly go back for more, even if it was a different woman dealing the cards this time.

Nope.

"—Amazing!" came Lauren's voice. "Show them, Denae."

Oh. He'd missed the announcement.

Denae glanced at him — why him? — and hesitated.

He forced out a casual grin. She didn't affect him. He

wouldn't let her. "Sure. Show us." Then he could clue into what he'd missed. A guy needed to know what his friends were up to.

She could be his friend. They hung out in the same crowd, after all. They were more Kade's friends than his, typical of their entire lives when his little brother gathered friends like the Pied Piper, and Trevor tagged along. It had been easier than finding his own, with a mere eighteen months separating them. Only one grade apart in school.

Cheri stretched a hand toward Denae as though they could touch across the room. "Go ahead."

"Yeah, Denae." Garret nodded. "If you can do it at the talent show, there's nothing to fear from us."

Trevor narrowed his gaze at Garret. Was the ranchland newcomer sniffing around Denae? That would be good, right? Because Trevor wasn't getting involved with anyone. Still, thinking 'Go, Garret' immediately morphed to 'Go away, Garret.'

Yeah. This was going to be a problem.

Why didn't Trevor's face show anything?

Denae Archibald didn't let her gaze linger on the strong, silent oldest member of this group that had welcomed her in. She didn't need to stare at him to remember every plane of his angular face, every dip of the thick brows that shaded his dark eyes, the ever-present five o'clock shadow.

He was gorgeous enough to take her breath away, and he'd done so every time she'd seen him in the past ten months since she'd moved back to Saddle Springs where Dad had owned a ranch when she was a kid. She'd loved summers at Standing Rock, loved riding wild and free in the mountains, away from the bratty little half-brothers she got to leave behind at Mom's. Dad had sold that ranch to the Delgado family a few years ago and simply told Denae after the fact, as though it wouldn't matter that he'd ripped away her happy. He'd thought nothing of it, had no clue what the ranch meant to her.

Now Trevor Delgado lived alone in the sprawling ranch house she loved so much. She wasn't sure which was worse: imagining this particular man sprawled in front of one of the field rock fireplaces, or imagining the stately home with only one person in it.

Sometimes she thought he watched her in an interested sort of way but, if so, why didn't he make a move? She was a pure romantic, old-fashioned enough to think the guy should express interest first but, one of these days, she was going to take matters into her own hands and be what may.

Denae fumbled with her tablet until she found the portfolio she was looking for then handed it to Garret on her left without a word.

"Scroll through it," suggested Lauren. Lauren, who'd been with Denae through thick and thin since the move and even before.

Garret emitted a low whistle and glanced at Denae with an approving nod. "Nice work." He handed the tablet to Carmen, who handed it to Cheri, who handed it to Kade, who handed it to Trevor.

Denae held her breath. Would he see what she'd tried to capture in those photos? The essence of people's souls through their eyes, the beauty of each face, each body, even though not perfect by society's standards? What she wouldn't give to photograph Trevor. She'd shoot him outdoors, on his black gelding, that cowboy hat in place. She'd capture those dark, mysterious eyes.

The ones that looked at her now. Really looked at her, as though a piece of the photographer had found its way into the subjects and then into the viewer.

He dipped his head. "Definitely a talent." He passed the tablet to James's sister Tori who sat on the floor nearby, but his gaze returned to Denae.

She was caught. Couldn't avert her stare. All she could do was try to convey, somehow, that she was as aware of him as he seemed to be of her at that moment in time. *Ask me out, Trevor.* Could she beg that with her eyes without anyone else noticing?

He looked away, the connection severed.

"Do you do family sittings?" asked Cheri. "I've been after my in-laws to get new portraits done. We should update the Eaglecrest website, too."

Family sittings? Not usually, but if it meant getting Trevor in front of the lens, it might be worth it. "I'm sure we can work something out. Do you want to do it before or after the baby?"

Cheri's hand went to her belly. "I hadn't thought that

far. Maybe after, when spring has come to the ranch and the apple trees are in blossom."

Kade caressed Cheri's shoulder. "We'll have to schedule around Sawyer if we're doing family photos."

Right, the youngest Delgado. The rodeo cowboy who was rarely home. A guy who risked life and limb for an instant of glory held no interest for Denae. Not when there were men like Trevor, who worked hard every day, regardless of the weather, regardless of the praise, regardless of the loneliness.

Because a person couldn't spend so much time alone without being lonely, right? Denae would go nuts without people around. Her chosen career as a romance novel editor was solitary enough, even though she entered romantic, flower-strewn worlds where devoted couples overcame all odds to find their true love. Still, when she closed a manuscript, she was still in the tiny spare bedroom of her rented duplex with Shae's big brown puppy-dog eyes looking up at her.

Still without a love of her own.

**The Cowboy's Romantic Dreamer
is now available**

ABOUT THE AUTHOR

Valerie Comer lives where food meets faith in her real life, her fiction, and on her blog and website. She and her husband of over 35 years farm, garden, and keep bees on a small farm in Western Canada, where they grow and preserve much of their own food.

Valerie has always been interested in real food from scratch, but her conviction has increased dramatically since God blessed her with four delightful granddaughters. In this world of rampant disease and pollution, she is compelled to do what she can to make these little girls' lives the best she can. She helps supply healthy food — local food, organic food, seasonal food — to grow strong bodies and minds.

Valerie is a *USA Today* bestselling author and a two-time Word Award winner. She is known for writing engaging characters, strong communities, and deep faith laced with humor into her green clean romances.

To find out more, visit her website www.valeriecomer.com where you can read her blog, and explore her many links. You can also find Valerie blogging with other authors of Christian contemporary romance at Inspy Romance.

Why not join her email list where you will find news, giveaways, deals, book recommendations, and more? Your thank-you gift is *Promise of Peppermint*, the prequel novella to the Urban Farm Fresh Romance series.

http://valeriecomer.com/subscribe

Made in the USA
Las Vegas, NV
27 April 2021